A Mammoth Scare

A shape was emerging from the bracken at the bottom of the empty field. It was not a human form. It was bigger than a human, it was broader than a human, it was humped like a walking mound of hay, and it swayed back and forth.

"Whatever it is, that's not Pearl Hotchkiss on her way home from the store," muttered Sammy Grubb. Mike nodded. Stan gulped. Forest Eugene blanched.

Salim fainted dead away.

SIX HAUNTED HAIRDOS

BY GREGORY MAGUIRE

ILLUSTRATED BY ELAINE CLAYTON

HarperTrophy®

A Division of HarperCollinsPublishers

Harper Trophy® is a registered trademark of HarperCollins Publishers Inc.

Six Haunted Hairdos
Text copyright © 1997 by Gregory Maguire
Illustrations copyright © 1997 by Elaine Clayton
Reprinted by arrangement with Clarion Books,
a Houghton Mifflin Company imprint

Library of Congress Cataloging-in-Publication Data
Maguire, Gregory.
  Six haunted hairdos / by Gregory Maguire ; illustrations by Elaine Clayton.
    p.   cm.
  Summary: With the help of their favorite teacher, two rival clubs, the all-boy
Copycats and the all-girl Tattletales, stop trying to out-do each other long
enough to help the ghosts of a baby elephant and a herd of mastodons that
appear near their small Vermont town.
  ISBN 0-06-440720-9 (pbk.)
  [1. Animal ghosts—Fiction.   2. Ghosts—Fiction.   3. Clubs—Fiction.
4. Vermont—Fiction.   5. Humorous storires.]   I. Clayton, Elaine, ill.
II. Title.
[PZ7.M2762Si   1999]   99-17585
[Fic]—dc21   CIP

First Harper Trophy edition, 1999
❖
Visit us on the World Wide Web!
http://www.harperchildrens.com

This book is for Martha Walke,
who generously shared her Vermont with me.

Whose woods these are we think we know.
But this is now. Long years ago,
Was someone—something—here before us?
Before we came, who ruled the forest?

CONTENTS

I
A Migrating Ghost

"If you ever see a ghost," the boy told his friends in a whisper, "you must do three things. First, pinch yourself to make sure you're awake. Second, pinch the ghost to make sure it's real."

"That's only two things," said someone.

"If it pinches back," said Salim, "the third thing to do is run for your life."

The other boys nodded. It was fun to be in the tree house at sunset, talking about ghosts. No one was scared. You could hear Mr. Grubb hammering on the back porch. A hammer pounding was a nice safe sound.

"But did you ever *see* a ghost?" asked Sammy Grubb, whose tree house it was.

"Yes," said Salim.

"You're making it up," said Sammy Grubb.

"Oh, I tell the truth," said Salim. "I saw a ghost on the Air India jet coming from Bombay this summer. I had been in the washroom at the rear of the cabin. When I came out, the movie had started. Everyone in the smoking section was lighting up cigarettes."

The other six members of the Copycats club stared at him.

"Just then," Salim continued, "the pilot spoke over the intercom. He said for all passengers to buckle their seat belts. We were flying over the Himalayas, tallest mountains in the world. We were heading straight for turbulent winds."

"And?" said the boys in unison.

"As I stood there, a ghost appeared, formed out of cigarette smoke. It floated in the light from the in-flight video. The ghost made a shadowy shape against the screen, sort of like a legless man with a tapering tail. At first people laughed because they thought it was part of the show. But somebody said, 'It's a ghost!' And everyone began to scream."

"Then what?" The boys waited breathlessly. Sammy Grubb's mouth opened up so wide that his gum fell out onto the tree house floor. He brushed the dirt off with his thumb and popped the gum back in his mouth. He wasn't scared of a little dirt. Besides, he needed to chew. That's how anxious he was.

Salim went on. "The jet hit an air bump and people screamed again. Chicken curry went globbing through the air, followed by a thousand grains of rice. The ghost stretched out something like a long thick arm, pointing toward the back of the cabin. An old granny screeched, 'We're all going to die!'

and then she fainted. But I thought the ghost was pointing at me."

The boys began to wish they had more than a single candle burning in their tree house. The evening was getting a bit too dark, and Mr. Grubb had finished his hammering and gone inside. "Then what?"

"The airplane bucked and stumbled on the currents like a fish flopping around on the bank of a river. The ghost began to swarm over the heads of everyone sitting in economy class. People ducked. I thought I should slip back into one of the washrooms, but they were all occupied. I was trapped!"

"And then?" asked Sammy Grubb, Chief of the Copycats club.

"And then?" echoed the other loyal members, Hector, Stan, Moshe, Mike, and Forest Eugene.

"There was no place to go!"

"And then?"

"When she fainted, the old granny leaned against the buttons in the arm of her seat, and she accidentally rang the bell for the steward. So, ghost or no ghost, an Air India steward came leaping bravely down the aisle. He yelled at me to get to my seat. Then he leaned over the granny to see what she wanted. He thought she was just asleep, so he opened an overhead luggage compartment to find her a complimentary Air India blanket."

"*And then?*"

"The ghost came floating nearer and nearer. If it was coming for me or the old woman, I couldn't say. But just then the airplane slid into a pothole in the

3

air and everything in the cabin jumped around again: babies, more chicken curry and rice, little airplane pillows, me—and also the smoky ghost. It was jostled upward into the open overhead luggage compartment. The steward slammed the door shut. Everyone cheered. We had a quiet trip all the way to London, where we had a stopover before changing planes for Boston. But the steward said that nobody should open that overhead compartment until all the passengers were safely off the plane."

"Who do you think the ghost was after? You?" asked Sammy Grubb.

"I don't know," said Salim. "When the granny came to her senses, she began to shriek that it was the ghost of her dead husband coming to haunt her. But when we landed in London her husband met her in the arrival hall, and then she remembered that he wasn't dead yet."

"I wonder where the ghost is now," said Sammy Grubb.

"Who can say?" said Salim. "Air India flies to many cities. But if a ghost ever shows up, remember the three things I told you to do."

"Number one: Pinch yourself to make sure you're awake," said Sammy Grubb.

"Right," said Salim.

"Number two: Pinch the ghost to make sure it's real," said Sammy Grubb.

"Right," said Salim.

"Number three: If the ghost pinches back," said Sammy Grubb, "run for your life."

"Right," said Salim. "But there's not very far away you can run if you're in an airplane."

Overhead, a jet airliner floated in the inky night like a spirit drifting among the stars. The Vermont woods nearby seemed dense with shadow and alive with suspicious sounds.

"What's that in the woods?" Sammy Grubb suddenly screamed. "Look! Down there!"

"It's a ghost!" Salim whispered. "Everybody, pinch yourselves!"

They all did. "Ow," said Sammy Grubb.

"Pinch the ghost!" said Salim. But nobody threw himself out of the tree house to do it. Down below, the figure in the woods came a little nearer.

"Anybody tries pinching me, they'll get more than a pinch back," said a voice.

"Oh," said Sammy, "it's Pearl Hotchkiss. What are you doing, spying on us?"

"I'm on my way home from the store," said Pearl. "I take the shortcut through Foggy Hollow. What's all this about pinching ghosts, anyway?"

The boys didn't want to admit to Pearl that they'd just gotten a little scare. "Oh, ghosts," said Sammy Grubb in a casual way, "we're just fooling."

"I wasn't fooling," said Salim. "I don't fool around about ghosts. And you better not either, if you know what's good for you."

"I'll watch my step," said Pearl and continued along the path home.

"What a brave girl she is," said Salim, "out in the woods alone at night. Doesn't she believe in ghosts?"

The boys didn't know. They didn't want to stick around to discuss it, either. It was getting too dark and scary.

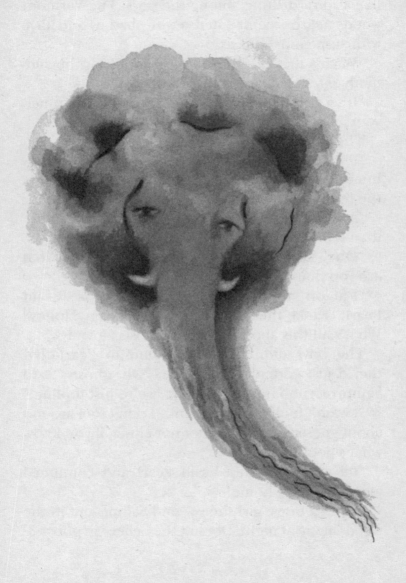

2
Boomtown

On the hillside behind the Josiah Fawcett Elementary School in Hamlet, Vermont, fall was on display. A few last red and orange leaves were still on the trees, and the fields looked brown and bare. Cold weather had come in overnight, so Hamlet parents had rooted in closets for thicker jackets and scarves. The air was rich with the smell of mothballs.

Teachers arrived carrying armloads of paperwork and books. Parents waved good-bye at little ones who forgot to wave back. Children ran shrieking happily in the schoolyard as if psycho ax murderers were after them. It was a normal November morning.

Salim Bannerjee was amazed to find that his breath was coming out of his mouth in steamy white puffs. "Look!" he said to his new friends. "I'm making little ghosts!"

"Didn't you have winter in Bombay?" asked Sammy Grubb.

"Not like this." Salim shivered in his cotton sweater.

"This is *nothing*," said Hector Yellow. "This is just the beginning of winter. You'll freeze your butt off!"

"Indeed?" said Salim with interest. But before he could learn more, the school bell rang and the children marched into the building.

Salim's teacher, Miss Germaine Earth, was the nicest teacher in the whole school. When Salim had told her he was new in the United States because his family had just moved from India, Miss Earth had smiled warmly. She replied, "Well, then, I speak on behalf of more than two hundred fifty million Americans when I say, 'Pleased to have you with us!'" The next day she rode on her Kawasaki 8000 Silver Eagle motorcycle to his house. She delivered a freshly made cake to Salim, his baby sisters, and his parents. The cake said WELCOME TO THE U.S.A.! on it in pink frosting. Salim's mother took a snapshot of it to mail back to Bombay so that everyone there could see it.

This morning, Miss Earth was just about to take attendance. Her students were sitting in respectful silence, hands folded on their desks, when a huge *boom* thundered outside. The glass in the window frames shivered. The venetian blinds rattled. The two new gerbils, named George and Martha, hid in their wood shavings as if praying for something to save them.

"What was that?" Salim was so startled he spoke

out loud without raising his hand. Across the aisle, Thekla Mustard shot a disapproving look at him. Her own hand zoomed into the air like a missile.

"Yes, Thekla?" said Miss Earth.

"Salim just spoke without raising his hand for permission," complained Thekla.

"Sometimes that happens, Thekla. Learn to tolerate small surprises in life. Now, Salim, were you startled by that noise? Who can tell Salim what it was?"

The children in Miss Earth's class were stuffed with imagination. They loved a question that prodded their minds to work. Each child liked to try to outdo the others. Fifteen eager hands waved back and forth like the twitching limbs of trees in a November gale. One by one Miss Earth called on her students, to hear what their ideas were about that huge noise.

Forest Eugene Mopp said, "It was a sonic boom!"

Nina Bueno said, "It was a thunderclap!"

Carly Garfunkel said, "An avalanche in Montreal!"

Hector Yellow said, "A Mack truck on Interstate 89 colliding with a moose!"

Sharday Wren said, "A meteor mashing Montpelier!"

Fawn Petros said, "A bomb blasting Bennington!"

Anna Maria Mastrangelo said, "A hippo falling off the Empire State Building!"

Stanislaus Tomaski said, "A whale with a bad case of the burps!"

Lois Kennedy the Third said, "The Statue of

Liberty burning her fingers on her lamp and dropping it!"

Mike Saint Michael said, "The Statue of Liberty burning her fingers on her lamp and dropping it on *Godzilla!*"

Moshe Cohn said, "King Kong stubbing his toe on the World Trade Center!"

"Very clever, very zesty," said Miss Earth, "though a bit off the mark. Any other ideas?"

Sammy Grubb stood up. Because Sammy was Chief of the Copycats, a club that all the boys in the class belonged to, it was important to the boys that his answer be the right one. Sammy said, "It's the sound of TNT explosives in the marble quarry up by Old Man Fingerpie's farm." The Copycats grinned in relief, even Salim, the newest member.

Thekla Mustard raised her hand for permission to speak. When Miss Earth nodded, Thekla stood and remarked in a clear voice, "More precisely, dear Miss Earth and fellow students, it's the *pressure* of airwaves against our thirty-two eardrums that makes such a noise." Thekla was the Empress of the Tattletales club. All of the girls in the class except one were Tattletales. Thekla Mustard believed it was her duty to correct any boy at any time. She liked to reassert the natural superiority of girls. Her loyal club members all grinned at her correct answer.

Pearl Hotchkiss was the only child in the class who didn't belong to a club. She was a rogue and a freethinker. She said, "Nobody asked me, but *I* think it's a ghost."

"Oh, Pearl!" said Thekla Mustard. "There aren't any such things as ghosts!"

"There are too," said Sammy Grubb. And then the room erupted into a loud discussion. While Miss Earth took attendance, she let the argument rage. When she was through, she rapped her little bell for silence. Her class shut up in the middle of a dozen sentences.

"We have a lot to do today," said Miss Earth, "but I confess that I, too, am curious. Why do you think it's a ghost, Pearl?"

"Because on Halloween last week," said Pearl Hotchkiss, "when I was trick-or-treating, I thought I saw a ghost coming around the corner of Old Man Fingerpie's farmhouse. The ghost was thick as a boa constrictor and milky white. I was standing there with my bag of candy and the ghost reached down looking for something. It found a couple of peanuts in their shells and the peanuts floated up in the air out of the bag! The ghost didn't actually eat them, just dropped them on the porch."

"Maybe it was Old Man Fingerpie?" proposed Miss Earth.

"That's what I thought, but when I got home I mentioned it to my folks," said Pearl. "They said that Old Man Fingerpie is in Florida until next April. No one stays in his house while he's away."

"What did you do?" said Sammy Grubb.

"I ran like the wind," said Pearl.

"And you never told anyone else until now?" said Thekla Mustard scornfully.

"I forgot. You know how exciting Halloween was," said Pearl.

"Well," said Miss Earth, "this is very interesting, but for safety's sake, I suggest that no one go to Old Man Fingerpie's house until next spring. Just in case. Not that I am sure there are such things as ghosts," she continued.

"Of course there are ghosts!" cried Sammy Grubb.

"You really think there are ghosts?" said Miss Earth. "Phantoms? Specters? Poltergeists?"

"Yes indeedy, Miss Earth."

"Apparitions? Wraiths? Shadies of the night?"

"You said it, Miss Earth."

"Astral spirits from the Great Beyond?"

"Even beyond *that*, Miss Earth."

Miss Earth bit her knuckle. "Horrors," she murmured.

"*Exactly*," said Sammy Grubb, and sat down. His Copycat comrades clapped. The Tattletales sat on their hands as if they were afraid their hands might start applauding by themselves.

But Thekla Mustard had shot to her feet now. "You mustn't fall victim to Sammy Grubb's superstitions! After all, Miss Earth, he's a boy, what does he know about the Great Beyond? He doesn't even know anything about the Great Here and Now!"

"I resent that," said Sammy. "I do too. And the Great Here and Now includes ghosts. How many kids believe in ghosts?"

All the boys and Pearl Hotchkiss—seven Copycats

and one independent—raised their hands. Eight votes in all.

"That's eight believers, here and now," said Sammy Grubb.

"Who *doesn't* believe in ghosts?" asked Thekla Mustard hotly. All the girls except Pearl Hotchkiss raised their hands. Seven Tattletales and an undecided teacher—Miss Earth raised her hand halfway.

"See! Boys are superstitious," cried Thekla. "So is Pearl."

"Girls are closed-minded," cried Sammy Grubb. "*Except* for Pearl."

Pearl started to blush. She liked Sammy Grubb. That's why, last night, she had taken the path home from the store that led through the woods near his back yard. But she didn't want her crush on him to show—not last night, not today. So she pretended she had to remove her sweater. She sat with her head stuck inside the sweater, which was halfway on and halfway off, until she could feel the blush was gone.

"Now, now," said Miss Earth. "How many times have I asked you not to make such broad remarks? It's simply not true that boys are one way and girls are another. We are all individuals, precious and unique."

"Miss Earth," snapped Thekla Mustard, "you know how it goes. What are little boys made of? Snips and snails and puppy-dog tails, that's what little boys are made of. And what are little girls made of?" continued Thekla, getting to the good stuff. She fluffed up her hair expectantly. "Sugar and spice and everything nice, that's what little girls are made of!" Thekla sat down with a satisfied *thwump*.

"Oh please," said Pearl Hotchkiss, rolling her eyes. "Let me outa here."

"What are little girls *really* like?" said Sammy Grubb in a dangerous voice. "The untold story!"

Hector Yellow, who was the most creative boy in the class, leaped up and said:

Fussing with makeup and hairdos and clothes!
Shopping and gossip and soap-opera shows!
Never believing in real things like ghosts
Unless they appear right in front of their nose!

"Them's fighting words!" yelled Thekla Mustard. "What are little boys *really* like? Somebody, quick, back me up on this!"

Anna Maria Mastrangelo lunged to her feet and recited:

Monsters and bloodthirsty crazies with knives!
Boys like to be scared right out of their lives!
Fighting and kicking like half-maddened ninjas!
Believing in ghosts! Boys are off of their hinges!

"I propose," said Thekla Mustard, "that believing in ghosts is just plain crazy. It's another proof, as if one were needed, that nothing's dumber than a boy! All in favor, scream with joy! Hip hip—"

"That'll do," said Miss Earth. "This has been interesting, but once again my class has divided along the fault lines of boyhood and girlhood. I do not approve. When will you ever learn? We are all individuals, all unique, all precious."

She smiled at them. They sat there beaming, each student trying to look more precious and unique than the next.

Miss Earth did love them fondly. As she admired them for their youthful zest, she remembered her favorite country-and-western song, the one sung by the Nashville singer named Petunia Whiner. The song went like this:

> *Blizzards snow, tornadoes blow,*
> *Ingrown toenails come and go.*
> *Troubles grow, but even so,*
> *Girl, here's what you gotta know:*
> *Stick with your man!*

Only sometimes Miss Earth changed the last line to say:

> *Stick with your kids!*

Miss Earth was a good teacher and a warm-hearted woman. However, she couldn't carry a tune to save her life, so it was lucky she hadn't gone into the music business. Happy with her career of molding young lives, she said, "Now, class, we'll have to continue this discussion of ghosts some other time. Right now the fine art of fractions requires our attention."

The class grumbled out of habit as they got out their math books. Outside, the peace of rural Vermont was shattered by another colossal *boom.*

"*I* believe in ghosts," said Salim Bannerjee almost under his breath.

"So do I," said Pearl Hotchkiss. "*Something* took those peanuts from me."

3
A Ghost Appears

Grandma was Grandma Earth. She was Miss Earth's mother. She wasn't really a grandmother because Miss Earth, her only child, was unmarried and childless. But everyone called Grandma Earth Grandma because she looked like one. She had a froth of grandmotherly white curls spilling off her head. Her eyes were poor. Her teeth were yellow. Her elbows dimpled like crumpled silk.

Grandma Earth was famous for making delicious doughnuts. People sometimes drove all the way from Montreal for them. If the customers' cars happened to break down in Hamlet, Vermont, Grandma Earth could help. She was a whiz at auto mechanics. She could wield a monkey wrench like a pro. She was as good with motor oil as she was with deep-fry oil. If she liked you, she'd leave a little package of doughnut holes on the front seat when you came to pick up your car. Her business was called Grandma's Baked Goods and Auto Repair Shop.

She turned down her CB radio and came in from the garage to take her place behind the bakery counter. Above the doughnuts was a wooden plaque showing a teapot and a cup, and the words TO TEA OR NOT TO TEA? THAT IS THE QUESTION.

"Well, boys, what'll it be?" she said to the Copycats, who had headed for doughnuts the instant school was out.

"The regular. Seven of them," said Sammy Grubb, speaking on behalf of all the Copycats. "Salim has never had one before."

"Poor soul," said Grandma Earth. She counted out seven of the best chocolate doughnuts in the known universe. Technically they were double-double-Dutch-Dutch-fudge-fudge-Swiss-Swiss-chocolate-chocolate-chocolate-chocolate doughnuts. Grandma called them chocolate swoons. "Seven chocolate swoons, coming up." The boys pooled their quarters and dimes, and Salim contributed two whole dollars. The boys devoured the doughnuts with gusto.

"Now whenever you order my chocolate swoons, it means you need extra special brainpower for something," said Grandma. "What're the Copycats up to today?"

Sammy Grubb wondered if Grandma Earth might have an open mind about ghosts. But weren't the elderly sometimes feeble and easily terrified? While he was thinking about it, a customer called from inside the garage, "Got my pickup ready yet, Grandma?"

"Chill out, hold your bladder, I've got customers," roared Grandma through the door. "Don't you know this is Vermont, the home of delayed gratification?" She looked seriously at the boys. "Anything on your mind that I can help you with, fellows?"

"No," said Sammy Grubb, though he was tempted. Whatever else Grandma Earth was, feeble and easily terrified she was *not*. "The doughnuts are help enough. Come on, guys."

They tramped back outside into the crisp November afternoon air.

"Hey, I got an idea," said Forest Eugene. "Let's show Salim the old swimming hole. Maybe if we're lucky we can feel an explosion close up." Since Salim was the new boy in the class this year, the Copycats were still having fun showing him the hidey-holes and shortcuts and secret lookouts of Hamlet, Vermont.

"I think I feel an explosion right here," said Salim, holding his stomach. He wasn't very used to chocolate.

The other boys were already yelling and cantering away, the thrill of the old swimming hole drawing them.

The light was golden brown and the hills gray, and the Copycats ran like young bucks out Squished Toad Road, past Old Man Fingerpie's place, and up the slope of Hardscrabble Hill. Twenty minutes later, belching chocolate gas, they came to a halt on the edge of the old quarry.

Hamlet marble was famous. A hundred years ago

the husky men of Hamlet had started carving marble from the hills, slicing it out in huge blocks. Hamlet marble had gone to sheath the capitols of several midwestern states. Once a well-known sculptor in Boston had carved something scandalous out of Hamlet marble, and the sculptor had been tarred and feathered and run out of town. Once a piece of Hamlet marble had fallen off the cornice of a Manhattan skyscraper and flattened a baby carriage just seconds after an Irish nanny had picked up Baby to burp it. That's what folks said, anyway. Hamlet marble led an interesting life, after twenty million years of waiting.

There was a new quarry being worked now, on the far side of Hardscrabble Hill. On the near side, the old played-out quarry had filled up with water. In winter it was an ice-skating rink. In the spring the slope was too muddy to climb this high in the hills. In summer the quarry became a perfect swimming hole, so deep that you could cannonball from any ledge in safety, although it was so cold that if you dove in the shadows you might get frostbite even in August.

In the fall, the old quarry pool was a wonder of nature. Birch trees had grown up around the pond, leaning over it so that their white reflections looked pasted onto black paper. This afternoon there was a pattern of red leaves, floating brilliantly on the water's skin like the bloody tracks of a beast escaped from a trap.

"Wow," said Salim reverently.

"You said it," murmured Mike. Salim's friends were pleased he was properly impressed. "Bet you never saw anything in India like this."

"Well, no," said Salim. He began to say what he *had* seen, but the boys weren't listening. They were trying to sink the crimson leaves with stones. The missiles made little plunking sounds and stirred up circles and rings on the water's surface.

"Don't get too near the edge," warned Sammy Grubb, feeling as he always did some responsibility for the Copycats. After all, he was the Chief. "If the quarriers detonate their explosives again this afternoon and you tumble in, you'll be a frozen Popsicle before we get you out."

The boys moved back about an eighth of an inch and kept pitching stones. They were loud with friendly competition. None of the boys was good at it, but it was fun to try.

Suddenly Stan said, "Hey, was that thunder?"

"If it is, it must be in Canada," said Forest Eugene. You could barely hear it.

"Well, what was it?" asked Salim. "Was it one of those TNT explosions?"

"An explosion this close, we'd hear," said Forest Eugene in a teacherly way. Forest Eugene was known as Mr. Science. "Don't forget, the active quarry is just on the other side of Hardscrabble Hill."

"There it is again."

They stopped throwing stones. The water began to soothe itself. Yes, there was a sound—a kind of low humming, a persistent rumble. It wasn't skyward, was it? They all looked up. Maybe it came through the ground? They looked down.

"Or," said Forest Eugene, puzzling, "is it from the pond? Water carries sound waves well, doesn't it? Whales can hear each other across the South Pacific from five miles away or more."

The boys stared at the water. It had a strange, hesitant look, as if it wanted to come to a simmer in tight efficient bubbles. For all that, Sammy noticed, the water wasn't moving—it was as still as a mirror.

A mirror.

"Look," said Sammy in a whisper. "Look in the water. The reflection—look."

They stared. It took a few seconds to focus.

Something was there. Something was hovering. They could see it reflected upside down in the water, drifting, formless. The last ripples from their stone-throwing contest still ruffled the skin of the water, so the thing hovered, shapeless as a dream. "Copycats," said Sammy Grubb, "what in nature or out of it *is* that thing?"

But before the water could settle down to be a perfect mirror, the men on the other side of the slope set off the last blast of the afternoon. All at once, the thing was gone.

"It reminds me of the ghost in the airplane," said Salim in a trembling voice. But the chocolate doughnuts were making him feel too queasy to talk, and later on he was no longer sure. So he didn't say any more.

4
The Tattletales
Have a Brainstorm

Across town, the Tattletales were having a meeting. Thekla Mustard was the Empress of the Tattletales, and the meeting was at her house. She sat cross-legged on her canopy bed like the queen of Sheba. The other girls were sprawled on the bubble gum pink–carpet. They looked as if they were lounging in a square puddle of Pepto-Bismol.

"I should like to call this meeting to order," said Thekla. "Shall I take attendance?"

"We're all here, Thekla," said Lois Kennedy the Third. Lois hated that Thekla always got voted Empress, so Lois enjoyed working hard to be a constant pain in Thekla's imperial neck. "All seven of us are here," said Lois. "What's this meeting all about anyway?"

"In class today," said Thekla, "the Copycats presented us with a perfect opportunity to prove, once and for all, that girls are superior to boys. We'd be lazy lumps if we didn't take advantage of it."

The girls didn't know what she meant. Fawn yawned and began to tease her hair with a comb until she looked like a double helping of cotton candy, complete with braces.

"Allow me to explain," said Thekla. "The boys today admitted that they believe in ghosts. Did you ever hear anything more ridiculous in your lives?"

"Boys are such infants," said Sharday Wren.

"Such babykins," said Nina Bueno.

"Get out the pacifiers," said Anna Maria Mastrangelo.

"Heat up the baby formula," said Lois Kennedy the Third.

"Buy some extra large Pampers," said Carly Garfunkel.

"Boys are so pea-brained," said Fawn Petros, working her hair to a froth.

"Today," said Thekla, "we are faced with a great chance both to scare the boys and to show them how ridiculous they are. I mean, really! Ghosts! That's like believing in the Tooth Fairy!"

"*I* believe in the Tooth Fairy," said Fawn.

They all stared at her hopelessly.

"Look, when you got braces, you gotta believe in something," said Fawn in a small voice. "The Tooth Fairy puts fifty cents under my pillow every Saturday night as long as I have these stupid braces on. Don't knock it."

Thekla tried hard to be kind. Since she had had so little practice at this, she flubbed it. "Fawn, you little idiot, the Tooth Fairy is your mother or father. Grow up."

Fawn ran from the room. She sobbed in the bathroom as if she'd just learned that the Tooth Fairy had been drilled to death by an insane dentist.

"Thekla," interjected Lois, "your being elected Empress doesn't give you permission to be nasty."

Thekla believed the proper thing to do with Lois was ignore her, so that's what Thekla did. She continued speaking as if Lois hadn't interrupted. "Here's my idea," said Thekla. "Let's dress up as ghosts and haunt those boys. They'll be scared out of their pants! And then we'll laugh good and hard when we tell them it was just us."

"But how do we haunt them?" asked Carly.

"I have the vision thing; you work out the details," said Thekla loftily. "Have a brainstorm, girls. Throw out some ideas."

"Boys like psycho murderers," said Nina. "They like chainsaw massacres and stuff like that. Could we be a ghostly chainsaw chain gang?"

"Too bloody," said Thekla. "Let's not stoop to their level of crudity. We *are* girls, after all, noted for our high-class manners and better brains."

"How about alien monster ghosts?" said Anna Maria. "We could be green slimy phantoms from another universe."

"Costumes of slime are hard to get hold of," said Thekla. "We could check at that store over in the Ethantown Mall—what's it called?"

"The Slime of Our Lives," said Carly. "No, they

don't have slime costumes. I know because my sister works there and I went to look. I wanted to be Slime Sister for Halloween, but I couldn't find a costume. I have an idea, though. Why don't we dress up as the ghosts of the seven Siberian snow spiders who terrorized us last month?"

"The ghost of a spider? Interesting," said Thekla. "Possibly. We'd have to cover ourselves with lengths of white gauze, which I think I could get from my dad's shop. But perhaps a white ghostly spider the size of one of us would look like a small shrub covered with snow. On the whole, we don't care to look much like small shrubs. Except for Fawn, when she teases her hair that way."

"Well," said Lois, "with all due respect, Thekla, I think we're barking up the wrong tree. I think we should punish those boys for the stereotyped way they think about girls. Did you hear what they said? Gossip and soap operas and fussing with clothes? Not me. Nor, by the way, am I sugar and spice and everything nice, as you paint us girls." She stuck out her tongue and crossed her eyes and made a gross sound by sticking her right hand up in her armpit and squeezing her arm down. The girls all cheered and clapped, except for Thekla, who was both insulted and upstaged.

But Thekla wasn't the Empress of the Tattletales for nothing. She could recognize a good idea when she heard one.

"Maybe you have a point, Lois," said Thekla. "The boys think we're fashion ninnies. They think we're simpering gutless bimbos. They think in stereotypes. Why don't we make fun of their old-fashioned ideas and scare them at the same time?"

"What are you talking about? Speak English, girl," said Sharday.

"Let's haunt those boys with their own images of us. Sugar and spice and everything nice! And what else did Hector Yellow say? Fussing with hairdos and makeup and clothes, shopping and gossip and soap-opera shows? Hah! Let's give them what they think we are and terrify them at the same time! We'll out-Dolly Dolly Parton!" Thekla Mustard was on a roll. "We'll be loud and rude and have hair the size of Mount Rushmore! We can pretend to be the ghosts of six ladies who got killed when their Vermont fall foliage tour minivan crashed into the quarry! We'll scorch them with those old-fashioned notions of girls as slaves to fashion! What do you say?"

Just then Fawn Petros came back from the bath-room. At first glance, it appeared that an attacking porcupine was standing upright on top of her head. But it was just that after she had finished crying she had teased up her hair some more.

"*Voilà!*" said Thekla, pointing at Fawn. "Exhibit A! She looks like the Bride of Frankenstein getting electrocuted! I rest my case!"

"I see it! I get it! We can be the Haunted Hairdos!" screeched Anna Maria. "We'll scare those boys bald!"

The vote was seven to nothing. Even Fawn voted to be a Haunted Hairdo, and she didn't even know what they were talking about.

5
Thunder and Frightenings

After school the next day, the Copycats stopped at Grandma's Baked Goods and Auto Repair Shop again. "Hi there, fellows," said Grandma, coming in from the middle of a lube job. "I hear that chocolate swoon doughnuts don't sit well in your stomach, Salim."

"I have a delicate Indian sensibility," said Salim. "May I try a plain cruller today?"

"One plain cruller and six chocolate swoons," ordered Sammy Grubb.

Again, Sammy Grubb wondered about asking Grandma Earth for advice about ghosts. Grandma Earth was the most sensible grownup in all of Hamlet, Vermont. However annoying the girls in the Tattletales club could sometimes be, Sammy knew that if girls could grow up to be great folks like Miss Earth or Grandma Earth, it was proof that girls were people, too. Actually, Sammy Grubb admired Thekla

Mustard. He didn't *like* her much; he just admired her. She was a smart cookie and a good leader. But Sammy both liked and admired Grandma Earth.

"Grandma Earth, did you ever see a ghost?" he said.

Just then Timothy Grass, the mayor of Hamlet, drove the town's snowplow into the garage. It was time for its annual checkup before the winter snows arrived. "Have I ever seen a ghost?" asked Grandma, rolling up her sleeves and slapping powdered sugar off her hands. "That old snowplow actually died back in 1946, and only prayers and the spirit of elbow grease keep it clanking. I could push snow off the roads better with a spatula and a pastry knife. I'd say this snowplow is a ghost of its former self." She headed into the garage to grouse happily with Mayor Grass.

Sammy Grubb sighed and passed the doughnuts out to his gang.

The wind was picking up again. The boys dropped off some overdue books at the library. Then they went to play football scrimmage in Hector Yellow's back yard. After a while they stopped passing and tackling and piling up on one another. They began to kick the ailing pigskin into the air.

"Watch," said Moshe, who had strong calf muscles. He connected with a *wump* and the football spiraled dizzily up. The boys circled beneath to try to catch it. They all felt an electrical crackle in their hair and ears even before they saw the splitting sword of lightning dance out of the sky.

"Outa here!" they chorused. They ran toward Hector Yellow's back porch and barely made it before the rain began.

To describe the storm as sheets of rain is to make it sound too thin, like parallel edges of rain with parallel spaces in between. No, it was almost solid water, dumping out of the sky like a waterfall. Within a few minutes the field had turned into a brown lake. Whenever the lightning struck, the thunder resounded at the same time, so the boys knew the center of the storm was very near indeed.

"Maybe we should go inside," said Hector, who had a fear of being struck by lightning. Even on the porch they were getting soaked to the skin by the gusting of the wind.

"This is great! This is almost like being on a ship at sea," said Stan.

"It's like the monsoon season in India," said Salim excitedly. "The rain comes down, you can set your watch by it, and—"

"Look!" cried Sammy, in his Chief-of-the-Copycats voice. All heads turned to where Sammy was pointing.

A shape was emerging from the bracken at the bottom of the empty field. It was not a human form. It was bigger than a human, it was broader than a human, it was humped like a walking mound of hay, and it swayed back and forth. It seemed to be looking around. Was the rain splashing off it, or was the rain filling in its outlines?

Another bolt of lightning was torn out of the sky

and dashed nearby, so close that the boys' eyeballs felt stewed. For a brief second it was as if they could see the x-ray of the world: all the blacks gone white, all the whites gone black. Though dark and apparently solid, the shape was transparent enough for the bony outlines of trees to show through it.

"Whatever it is, that's not Pearl Hotchkiss on her way home from the store," muttered Sammy Grubb. Mike nodded. Stan gulped. Forest Eugene blanched. Moshe bit his lip. Hector bit his fingernail.

Salim fainted dead away. By the time they dragged him into the kitchen and slammed the door behind them, the power had gone off and the room was plunged into darkness.

6
The Rain of Terror

The rain stepped up. The wind was howling like a saber-toothed tiger. Upstairs, a shutter blew loose and smashed, again and again, against the side of the house.

"The power's out," said Forest Eugene, as if they hadn't all noticed.

"The phone's dead," said Stan, returning the receiver to the cradle.

"I got a walkie-talkie for my birthday—" began Hector.

"Hooray!" they all cried.

"But my dad ran over it when I left it in the driveway," he finished.

"The thing is still out there," said Moshe.

"Maybe it's not a ghost?" said Hector in a small, hopeful voice.

"If that thing isn't a ghost," said Moshe, "I don't know what it is. What else could an almost invisible formless form be?"

"Don't panic," said Sammy Grubb, trying to keep his friends calm. "Let's not assume anything."

"Ghosts," said Forest Eugene in his best Mr. Science voice, "are the spiritual residue of unhappy creatures. Ghosts rattle chains and moan in pain. They generally suffer in a public way. It stands up to scientific scrutiny to suppose," concluded Forest Eugene, "that this visitor is a ghost and that it is not approaching the house to borrow a cup of sugar. I rest my case."

"Well, you may be right," said Sammy Grubb glumly. "I don't know what we can do. I'd say make a run for it, but we can't leave Salim here."

"We have nothing to defend ourselves with!" shrieked Mike, who was looking out the window. "It's coming this way! What do we do now?"

"I have a mouse," said Hector. "He's called Jeremiah Bullfrog. Don't ask me why, some song I apparently liked when I was a baby."

"Oh great, an attack mouse," moaned Mike. "I can just see the headlines now. In the picturesque little village of Hamlet, Vermont, seven grade-school boys and a mouse were killed today by a rampaging ghost. The boys' bodies were found in bloody disarray behind the corpse of one Jeremiah Bullfrog, who valiantly died defending the boys. The mouse was buried with full military honors, with the open safety pin he'd used as a weapon still clenched in his mouth."

"Shut up!" screamed Stan, looking out the window. "It's coming closer!"

Sammy looked at the window and saw the shape lumbering forward. "Bring out the mouse!" he said briskly.

Hector thought Sammy was crazy, but Sammy *was* the Chief of the Copycats, and so Hector scurried to obey. The mouse lived in a cage in his bedroom, and Hector hurried through the shadowy rooms. "Wake up, Jeremiah Bullfrog," he crooned softly, touching him with his finger. "Your hour of triumph is at hand."

In the kitchen, the boys stayed crouched down, their noses propped up on the windowsills, looking. The thing was coming closer. "It *is* a ghost—but of what?" said Forest Eugene in a whisper.

The shape sloped this way and that. The rain seemed to run off the thing even though it wasn't there, which made it look like a huge mound of silver strings. Bloblike, it leaned left, then right, as if correcting for balance. "It's looking for something," said Mike.

"It's heading this way," said Sammy, "and I don't think it's come to ask for directions to Brattleboro."

"Maybe it's attracted by the smell of doughnuts," said Forest Eugene.

Hector returned with Jeremiah Bullfrog, the little brown mouse. "He's a bit sluggish; he thinks it's nighttime," said Hector.

Forest Eugene and Stanislaus were both rubbing Salim's wrists to try to increase circulation. "Hurry up, Salim, wake up; we have to make a run for it," said Stanislaus. "Come on, come on!"

"The thing is coming near," said Sammy in a steady voice.

"Let's go down to the cellar," said Forest Eugene.

"It's picking up speed. Holy tornado!" cried Sammy.

There was a sudden slash of light and a smell of charred wood as the porch pillar split on one side. The thing was backing up, as if undecided. Then it began to move forward again.

"Everyone, hit the floor!" ordered Sammy.

They slammed onto the linoleum. As Hector was raising his forehead over the windowsill to look out, Salim began to come around. He clutched his throat and said, "Mamaji?"

"It's us, Salim," said Sammy Grubb. "Brace yourself. Either the ghost is attacking, or we're being hit by lightning. But lightning never strikes twice in the same place—"

"Wait," said Salim, blinking, "is this a mouse I see here?"

"That's Jeremiah Bullfrog," said Hector.

"I have an idea," said Salim. "Hector, may I try? In the interest of preserving our lives?" Hector nodded sorrowfully. Salim took the little brown field mouse in his hand. Salim ran a kindly finger along his trembling furry back and said to him, "Be brave, little brother, so that your bigger brothers can live to talk about it."

Then, without warning, Salim ran to the kitchen door. He said something in Hindi and put the mouse on the threshold. Jeremiah Bullfrog looked as if he didn't particularly want to venture out into the storm. However the appetite for freedom dies slowly, if it dies at all. Inside the house meant life in a cage, constant sleep, and a regular diet. Outside meant rain, wind, owls, foxes, snakes, cats, cold, and a ghost. Live Free or Die, as the motto of neighboring New Hampshire said. The mouse chose freedom and darted outside.

At the sight of Jeremiah Bullfrog, the apparition reared back, if it could be said to rear, and went lumbering away.

"I have an idea who this ghost is," began Salim, but the boys were so glad that the apparition had disappeared that they began to sing another country-and-western song that Miss Earth had taught them.

> *You took my heart when you went away,*
> *You took the keys to my Chevrolet,*
> *You took the dog tied in the yard,*
> *But did you have to take my library card?*

No one was listening to Salim, so he decided not to share his theory with them. For the time being.

7
The Legend of
the Six Lost Ladies

The day after the storm, Thekla Mustard was
ready to lay the trap for the Copycats. She was
good at this sort of thing. She raised her hand and
said, "Miss Earth? I have some unsettling news to
report."

"Oh my," said Miss Earth. She put down the
attendance book and said, "What is it, Thekla?"

"As you may know, my father is the owner of
Hamlet Eyewear, whose motto is To See or Not to
See? That Is the Question. As a maker of eyeglasses,
my father only believes in what he can see. But he
says that something has been haunting the quarry.
He thinks it's the ghosts of the six ladies who died in
that horrible accident. He thinks he saw them."

"What horrible accident?" asked Miss Earth.
Thekla noticed the boys listening with special
interest. Good! They were swallowing the bait!

"Oh, you remember," said Thekla. "That fall
foliage tour minivan that went off the road and

plummeted into the swimming hole in the old quarry?"

"I don't recall. How long ago did this happen?" said Miss Earth.

"I don't know exactly. The minivan sank with all aboard, and only the bus driver managed to smash his way through the windshield and claw his way to safety. The others were never seen again. They were six vacationing hairdressers, six ladies out to admire the glories of nature. May they rest in peace."

"What are you getting at, Thekla?" said Miss Earth. "Gripping this may be, but we have work to do."

"Well, my father doesn't believe in ghosts," continued Thekla. "But he said that one night when he was locking up his shop, he saw something swaying along the double yellow line on Route 12. He ran inside and got a pair of very special glasses and looked. It seemed to be six women struggling up the middle of the road. Six ladies who now consider the glories of nature from another point of view entirely. He said you could almost see through the ladies, as through the morning mist. They didn't look very happy."

"I wonder why," said Miss Earth.

"They didn't want to be dead," said Thekla Mustard. "My father ran back in his shop and locked the door."

"I know your father is an honest and a sensible man," said Miss Earth, "so if he said that he saw six shady ladies roaming up the middle of Route 12, I believe him. But I am reluctant to call them ghosts. Perhaps they were a trick of the light or the product of a runaway imagination."

"I mention this," Thekla concluded, "so that my classmates might be on the alert. Whether we believe in ghosts or not—and of course I still do not—we must be on the lookout for the ghosts of ladies who never got to finish their Vermont fall foliage tour."

Pearl Hotchkiss raised her hand. Miss Earth nodded, and Pearl said, "Thekla, why would you warn us about ghosts if you don't believe in them?"

"I don't believe that there is a monster living underneath the basement stairs," said Thekla, "but I still wouldn't send a sensitive young child down there to check. I am trying to express compassion for my fellow students, boys and girls alike."

Thekla glanced around. The boys looked pale. She didn't know it, but they were remembering the ghostly thing at Hector's house and the thing reflected in the old swimming hole. "Any other questions?" she asked, improvising.

Sammy Grubb said, "Thekla, where were these ladies from?"

"Oh," said Thekla, "they worked part-time for a beauty salon down in Massachusetts someplace. It was called Curl Up and Dye."

Sammy said in a small voice, "Maybe they don't like being ghosts."

"I wouldn't know," said Thekla jauntily. "I don't

even believe in ghosts. But I'm still going to watch out. Six lady hairdressers marauding around the village of Hamlet, Vermont, are a force to be reckoned with."

"But why should we be scared of them?" said Pearl.

"Did you ever hear of contented ghosts?" said Thekla. "No, ghosts always have some unfinished business. These hairdressers were cut off in their prime. They could be trying to decide whether to be or not to be. Or, put another way, whether to boo or not to boo."

"I will tell my mother," said Miss Earth, "even though I think she doesn't believe in ghosts either."

"Seeing is believing, that's all I'll say," said Thekla. She smiled like a deranged gorilla and sat down. Her work was done.

Pearl Hotchkiss had a scowl on her face. She smelled a rat. What was Thekla Mustard up to now?

When Miss Earth arrived home from school that afternoon, the CB radio was on, and truckers and homebodies were broadcasting back and forth to each other in a neighborly way. Miss Earth parked her Kawasaki 8000 Silver Eagle motorcycle in the garage next to the town snowplow. Her mother was bent over the motor, up to her elbows in spark plugs and engine grease. "Don't kiss me till I clean up, Germaine; you'll spoil your good clothes," said Grandma Earth. "How was your day?"

"Tiring but thrilling, as always," said Miss Earth. "Molding tiny minds is so rewarding." She turned down the CB radio and gave herself a little ride on the hydraulic lift. (She liked doing her thinking while elevated.) From eight feet up in the air she looked down at her mother fondly. "Today the big question in class," said Miss Earth, "was about the six ghostly women haunting Hamlet."

"Haven't heard of them," said Grandma Earth. "Who are they?"

"Six hairdressers from Massachusetts who died during a fall foliage tour."

"Poor souls. Hope it was a peak weekend, at least."

"Mother," said Miss Earth, "do you believe in ghosts?"

"I'm not sure," said Grandma Earth. "Us Yankee folks never did much believe in things you can't see. But you can't see wind, or gravity, or time, and *they* seem to be real enough. So do love and honor and a sense of humor. So maybe there are ghosts. What do you think?"

"I'd like to be sure one way or the other," said Miss Earth.

"I bet the boys in your class believe in ghosts," said Grandma Earth. "They've been in the shop every day this week. I can always tell when something's up. They look worried."

"I hate to see them worried," said Miss Earth. "I'd protect them from worry if I could." She began to sing her favorite country-and-western song.

Blizzards snow, tornadoes blow,
Ingrown toenails come and go.
Troubles grow, but even so,
Girl, here's what you gotta know:
Stick with your kids!

"It's all you can do," said Grandma Earth, brandishing a metric wrench. "Against ghosties and ghoulies and things that go bump in the night, stick with your kids."

8
The Dress Rehearsal

The next day, which was Saturday, the two clubs met on opposite ends of town.

The Copycats gathered in Sammy Grubb's tree house. They were discussing what they had seen—once on the edge of the quarry swimming hole, once outside Hector Yellow's house. Was it possible that they had met the ghostly remains of six poor women who had drowned during their autumn hunt for the glories of nature? All clotted together and moving as if one huge clump of hairdresser? If so, why would the ghosts of six hairdressers on vacation show up on Hector Yellow's back porch? It wasn't as if Hector's father ran a rival barbershop or anything. (The Copycats were still not sure if it was lightning that had struck the porch, or the insubstantial mass of a ghost.)

"I think it was lightning," Hector said. "How could a filmy, flimsy ghost buckle the pillar on a porch roof? Even if there were six of them bundled together?"

"It doesn't add up," said Sammy Grubb. "I didn't get the sense that there was more than one ghost there."

"Maybe when ghosts are ghosts, they're not so individual anymore," said Moshe.

"I think they're *just* as individual; otherwise they wouldn't be ghosts," said Sammy Grubb. "Otherwise they'd just boil down to be a kind of creepy atmosphere. No, a ghost is a ghost because it keeps itself intact. Precious and unique—just what Miss Earth says about us. That makes sense. But either that wasn't the ghosts that Thekla was talking about, or else one of those poor hairdressers has changed quite a bit since she was a living human being."

"I hate to interrupt," said Salim, "but it's my opinion that we didn't do the right thing."

"What do you mean?" Sammy Grubb asked him.

"Remember? I said that when you see a ghost, you should pinch yourself to see if you are awake."

"Yeah?"

"Well, I couldn't do that because I had fainted. Did anybody else try?"

They all shook their heads sheepishly.

"Next, you're supposed to pinch the ghost to see if it's real. Did you try that?"

Sammy Grubb said, "Are you kidding?"

Hector Yellow said, "Pinch that ghost?"

Stan Tomaski said, "I'd rather pinch Frankenstein!"

Mike Saint Michael said, "I'd rather pinch Godzilla!"

Moshe Cohn said, "I'd rather pinch Cruella De Vil!"

Forest Eugene Mopp said, "I'd rather pinch Thekla Mustard! Give me a break!"

"Besides, how can you pinch a ghost?" asked Mike. "What's to pinch? It's just air, isn't it?"

"It was my grandfather in India who gave me that advice," said Salim. "He never mentioned whether a ghost is actually pinchable or not. So don't ask me. I'm not the rocket scientist."

All the boys turned to look at Forest Eugene, who had his own subscription to *Nature* magazine.

"It's really quite simple," said Forest Eugene. He adjusted his eyeglasses so he could look over the tops of the lenses in an owlish, scholarly way. He loved to be asked science questions. "If I brought you a metal thermos filled with water and said, 'Empty it out in an hour without tipping it over or dropping anything into it,' could you do it?"

The boys all shook their heads no.

"Yes, you could," said Forest Eugene. "You'd just put it on a hot stove until the water evaporated. Now, think about this. If I brought you the same amount of water in a cookie tin and a bunch of cookies and said, 'Set these cookies on top of the water without submerging them or placing anything else between the water and the cookies,' could you do it?"

The boys all shook their heads again: No.

"Yes, you could," said Forest Eugene. "You'd just put the whole tin in the freezer. When the water had turned to ice, you could easily set the cookies on top without submerging them."

"Your point being?" said Sammy Grubb, making

a little circle in the air with his hand to suggest that Forest Eugene move along.

"H_2O is still itself whether it's in the form of water, steam, or ice," said Forest Eugene. "When it's steam, it can pass through the air unseen. When it's ice, it has mass and bulk. My theory is that a ghost is the same way, able to shift back and forth between states of being. Sometimes it is more flimsy, sometimes less so."

"Proof," said Moshe, who was something of a skeptic.

"Everyone knows that ghosts rattle chains and creak floorboards and sit in rocking chairs and rock them," said Forest Eugene. "How could ghosts do that without some kind of weight and force? On the other hand, ghosts can pass through walls and dissolve like mist. Clearly, ghosts can manifest themselves as different states of being. So sometimes there'd be something to pinch—and sometimes not. Depends, I bet, on the ghost's mood."

"Makes sense," said the boys to one another. Even Moshe shrugged and said, "Who knows? Why not? Beats me."

"I rather think that what we saw at Hector's house was a ghost," said Salim firmly. "I have some personal reasons. And I have a hunch I know who that ghost was. But I need to look a little closer to be sure. Tomorrow I'm going to go up on Hardscrabble Hill and look for the ghost. But I want to go alone. All I ask of you is one thing."

"What's that?" asked Sammy Grubb.

"If I am not back by five o'clock," said Salim, "call the state police. And Hector—I need to borrow Jeremiah Bullfrog."

"You can't," said Hector. "He ran away in the storm." Hector looked sad. The boys didn't mind it that he started to cry a little. They would cry too if their pet mouse had been lost in a campaign against the ghostly otherworld.

Across town, in Thekla Mustard's bedroom, the Tattletales were having a great time. They were constructing the ghosts of six imaginary ladies who died in the search for the glories of nature.

Fawn's mother had a whole closetful of wigs left over froms the 1960s. "Back when I was a little girl," Mrs. Petros had told Fawn, "having big hair was all the rage. The hairdos were called beehives. Ain't they something?" Mrs. Petros worked in a beauty salon called Hamlet House of Beauty. There was a sign in the shop window that said TO BEEHIVE OR NOT TO BEEHIVE?

Fawn had borrowed six huge wigs from her mother's collection. The first wig was a monstrous white froth like an exploding sheep. The second wig was honey-colored, and it spiked into points, like whipped cream that peaks stiffly when you put a knife in it. The third wig stood itself up vertically like a headful of bicycle spokes. The fourth wig was gathered high up by a ribbon and then crowned with a little ponytail sticking straight up. It resembled a tan plastic garbage bag all filled up and tied with a twist tie at the top. The fifth wig featured two braids long enough to jump rope with. The last wig looked a little bit like a gray tidal wave, sweeping back to front. It had real live moths living in it.

Thekla said, "I am not going to be one of the six lost ladies. I will be the plant who makes sure the Copycats know exactly what they're seeing. So come on, girls, let's try on that hair."

Fawn was the bravest. She went first. She tried on the wig that looked like an exploding sheep. Except that Fawn's hair was fawn-colored instead of white, the wig made her look just like herself. Nobody said anything, but everyone thought: This is what Fawn is going to look like when she's ninety-five.

Encouraged, the other girls selected wigs. Lois took the honey-colored spike bush. Anna Maria took the bicycle spokes. Carly took the tan garbage bag with the up-top ponytail. Sharday took the mammoth pigtails. And Nina took the tidal wave with moths sporting in the foam of the bangs.

"Six Haunted Hairdos!" screeched Thekla. "Girls, I love you!"

They laughed so hard they couldn't stand up. When they fell down, the hair didn't even get dented. The wigs seemed to have been sprayed with some aerosol type of steel.

"Now we need some good weird clothes," said Thekla, "so that the boys don't guess it's us. And we need some mood music."

"Why weird?" said Lois. "Wouldn't hairdressers wear ordinary clothes?"

"Lois," said Thekla, "for once, you're right. I was thinking zany, but perhaps we should rein ourselves in. Maybe if we all wore white pajamas or light gray skirts and sweatshirts. We might need to bleach the blues out of our jeans. Everybody go home and find what you can find. Get gauze, if you can; get talcum powder. Borrow white gloves from your mothers if you can. Carly, is your sister still working at that costume store? Here's what to ask for."

"What are you doing to do?" said Lois sulkily. "Almighty Empress of ours?"

"I'm going to sit here and try to figure out how we can lure the boys to a spot that would be frightening," said Thekla, "and how we can scare them out of their wits without giving ourselves away. Brainpower is hard work, Lois. You wouldn't know. Don't question me."

"You're not an empress," said Lois, "you're a dictator." But, like the others, she went home to hunt for an outfit suitable for a ghost with a huge head of hair.

By midafternoon the Tattletales returned. They brought shopping bags and knapsacks overflowing with supplies. "Can everything here can be ripped to shreds if need be?" asked Thekla, poised with a pair of pinking shears over a prom gown that looked

49

like something Scarlett O'Hara might have worn to the Battle of Bull Run. The girls nodded.

"On your mark, get set, create," proclaimed Thekla.

An hour and a half later the Six Haunted Hairdos were born. The Tattletales named themselves according to the look of the wig each one wore.

Fawn called herself Fawn the Inflammable Fleece. She wore a huge Cinderella-type white ball gown with puffs of lamb's wool pinned all over it, as if her dress had a bad case of woolly leprosy. She had put a cowbell around her neck and she carried a little hammer so she could strike the bell from time to time and *baa* her head off. "To baa or not to baa, that is the question!" she bleated.

"Lose the bell," said Thekla. "Otherwise, you're a genius." Fawn wasn't used to being complimented for being a genius. She grinned like anything over Thekla's compliment.

Lois was rather proud as Lois the Lounge Singer. She wore skin-tight leopard-skin pedal pushers and a white blouse featuring a huge fake frontage created by tissue paper. "You'll have to dye the pedal pushers; that gold-and-brown leopard skin is a real no-no," said Thekla, tutting. Lois stuck out her tongue at Thekla and put on a pair of ruby-colored cat's-eye glasses with pointy rims.

Anna Maria called herself Sister Anna Maria Spokehead. She wanted to be a nun in real life, so she had brought some white bedsheets and folded them around herself to look like an old-fashioned nun's habit. She had cut a bib out of white cardboard and pinned it to the front of the habit. She looked like a nun having a nightmare, with her hair standing straight up like that.

"I'm Carly the Trash Collector," said Carly as she pranced back and forth in white trousers and a white blouse with a huge tan sack of hair swaying dangerously up top. She had tied a dog's bone to the knot at the top of her head.

"A bit over the top," mused Thekla. "Maybe? Maybe not. We'll see."

Sharday had inserted two yardsticks into her long braids, and now they stood at attention on top of her head. "I don't know who I am, but I feel like Dorothy after the flying monkeys carried her away by her pigtails! Don't call me Sharday, call me Shar-Dorothay!"

Nina had on her white tae kwan do costume. "I'm Nina the Queen of the Marine Scene!" She wore the wig like the tidal wave, and in it she had festively pinned some wooden fish that were really Christmas tree ornaments.

And then, the crowning touch: Out of a bag, Carly pulled the six white skull facemasks that her older sister Paula had borrowed from the costume store over at the Ethantown Mall. The girls put on the masks. Lois managed to fit her ruby-colored eyeglasses over her mask. Thekla added finishing touches by draping them all with yards of white gauze and gray muslin. Then Thekla drifted among her subjects, sprinkling dollops of baby powder.

"You must appear wispy and ethereal, like real ghosts," she said.

"Real ghosts?" snapped Lois, who was always looking for an advantage over Thekla. "I thought you didn't believe that ghosts were real."

"You know what I mean," said Thekla. Sometimes Lois Kennedy the Third was an absolute pain.

"I hope we don't give the boys heart attacks," said Sharday. She looked worried. "I mean, wouldn't we be guilty of murder if one of them dropped dead of fright?"

"What a tender heart you have," said Thekla. "You'll have to get over that, Sharday."

"Sharday has a point," said Anna Maria. "A joke is a joke, but we don't want to hurt the boys."

"Don't worry," said Thekla. "We're out to embarrass them, nothing more. I'll be there with them to give them courage when they first catch sight of you. Now, on your mark, get set, go go ghosties!"

The Tattletales grinned and practiced being scary. Thekla watched and gave them notes on their performances. "You look wonderful, darlings," said Thekla. "Truly frightening. There's nothing quite so terrifying as hairstyles that have gone out of fashion." Then Thekla dismissed the Tattletales and made them go home. After she straightened up her room, neat as a pin, she got on her bike and zipped over to where Miss Earth and Grandma Earth lived. She needed to borrow a tape of Petunia Whiner singing "Stick with Your Man," and she knew Miss Earth had one.

While the Copycats were discussing the various shapes in nature that ghosts could take, and while the Tattletales were dressing up as ghosts, Pearl Hotchkiss was at the library. She was trying to get up the courage to ask Mr. Dewey about the accident with the minivan. He was the librarian; he knew everything. Or he knew how to find out. But just as she got up the nerve to bring the subject up, a handful of parents arrived with a mob of four-year-olds for story hour. Mr. Dewey told them a story called "The Ghost in the Toaster." It was a funny story and all the kids laughed, and so did Pearl. But it made her feel a little silly, so she ended up going home without asking for his help.

9
The Winds of Hardscrabble Hill

On Sunday, Salim took a small stick of incense and put it in his pocket. He kissed his parents good-bye and left the house. Even though it wasn't much like Bombay, he was starting to like Hamlet, Vermont. Fall had been spectacular, a blitz of hot Indian reds and yellows that had made him feel as if he were standing among mounds of colored spices at the Bombay marketplace. Winter, with its new experience of snow, was lurking just out of sight, a month or maybe even only weeks away. Salim sincerely hoped that he wasn't about to get mushed by an overexcited ghost. He wanted to be around to see snow for the first time in his life.

Salim had a feeling he knew who the ghost was. He hardly wanted to say it out loud to himself. But if the ghost was who he thought it was, Salim was to blame.

As he scuffled through heaps of brown crackling

leaves, he remembered the zoo at Bombay. He remembered a certain animal yard. A fat woman from Calcutta and all her fat relatives were standing by the iron fence, having their picture taken by a fat man. They were so fat that they blocked out everything behind them. When they moved away to go to the lion house, Salim saw a handwritten sign taped to the fence. It said PLEASE DON'T FEED BABY TUSKER. ITS MOTHER HAS DIED OF AN EVIL STOMACH VIRUS AND BABY TUSKER IS SICK TOO. But Salim had already tossed a whole sack of peanuts into the yard for Baby Tusker.

Baby Tusker was a cute little elephant—well, little for an elephant. Actually it was about the size of a compact car. It didn't look very sick. It reached out its trunk and felt Salim's face, looking for peanuts. Salim fell in love.

But then Baby Tusker found the peanuts Salim had thrown in the elephant yard. It began to snort them up. "Help!" cried Salim. "Elephant keepers! Park administrators! Governors of the zoo! Concerned citizens of India! Baby Tusker is eating peanuts!" By the time the animal doctor had come running, Baby Tusker had eaten every peanut.

"Don't worry," said the animal doctor, looking worried. "Perhaps Baby Tusker is over its virus by now. Do not be concerned, little boy. Run and play."

But a week later Salim's mother had read something awful in the newspaper. "Baby Tusker Yields Its Last Breath; Evil Virus Triumphs; Zoo Staff Mourns; Ten Thousand Zoo Visitors Riot in Grief."

When Salim had burst into tears, his mother had said, "It can't be helped, my darling, the elephant child was sick with the flu."

"It's all my fault!" cried Salim and told her about the peanuts.

"Nonsense," said his mother. "Peanuts have nothing to do with the flu."

But Salim could not be consoled. "You're crying because you're tired and because you're scared of moving to the United States," said his mother. She took him to the market to get him some pan to chew on. That was his favorite savory snack and it usually made him feel better. But that day the pan tasted like peanuts. "We'll always have each other," said Salim's mother, and when his father came back from the Air India ticket office he hugged Salim and his two baby sisters, too.

"Don't be sad, Salim," said his father. "If your mother doesn't like her new job at Locust Computer Labs in the United States, we will move back to India. Besides, we will come here to visit your granny and grandfather and your aunties next summer. Never fear. Of course you're sad for the baby elephant. But you still have a mother and a father and two baby sisters, and we love you and we won't die of peanuts or evil viruses, at least not for a very long time."

In the airplane, when the ghost had unrolled in front of the movie screen and had come streaming over the heads of passengers in economy class, Salim thought he recognized it. It was the ghost of

Baby Tusker. It was coming to find out why Salim had fed it peanuts when it was already feeling low with an evil stomach virus.

Salim hadn't wanted to tell his new friends about this. He didn't want to admit that he was guilty of accidental murder. Of course Salim realized that it wasn't exactly his fault. He couldn't help it if the fat family from Calcutta had stood right there in front of the sign. And Baby Tusker hadn't caught the flu from *him*. But even so. The peanuts had come from Salim's own hand, and the little orphan elephant had died.

And now it was looking for him.

So as Salim walked up Hardscrabble Hill, past Old Man Fingerpie's farm, heading for the swimming hole in the old quarry, he said to himself, "I must be brave enough to apologize to the ghost for feeding it peanuts. I hope it will accept my apologies and go off someplace else."

When Salim reached the old quarry, he sat down very still under a birch tree. The shape of the bark seemed like eyes, dozens of black-rimmed eyes looking in every direction. Salim felt safe there. "Come, Baby Tusker," said Salim. "Let me see you." He lit a stick of incense and stuck it in the ground.

For a long time nothing happened. Nothing was there except Salim, the birch tree, and about ten thousand other trees and bugs and leaves, as well as water and sky.

Then something changed. It was hard to say what it was.

"Baby Tusker?" Salim said.

Something hovered, like a huge tattered crab, like a bony-fingered hand, like a ragged claw. It was made by the wind out of dead leaves and twigs and litter. It didn't have a form of its own. The red maple leaves and brown oak leaves were like iron filings around a magnet, suggesting just an outline, a shape. It hung, swaying, descending, from a height of eight or nine feet.

It was about twice as big as Baby Tusker had been. If this really was the elephant child at the zoo, it was thriving in its afterlife.

"If you're Baby Tusker, I'm sorry for the peanuts," said Salim, holding up the incense stick. He hoped that some of the smoke would be sucked into the hollow space that swung nearer and nearer to him, so that he could see some detail—a tusk, a trunk, a flapping ear. But the incense stick didn't give off enough smoke to do the job.

It was coming nearer.

Salim swallowed hard. Was this the end? Had he come all the way from Bombay, India, to Hamlet, Vermont, just to be done in by a ghost? If this really was an elephant ghost, how would it take its revenge? It probably couldn't gore him with tusks. Maybe it would gum him to death with its mothy misty moisty mouth? Could ghosts do that? What a disgusting thought.

But before Salim could find out, there was a shuffle of something in the leaves near Salim's knees. Something tiny that hardly made any noise at all. Something pattered out from underneath some leaves and ran into the leaves at the foot of the apparition. Could it be Jeremiah Bullfrog?

The ghostly presence seemed to freeze at the rustle. Then it vanished.

Maybe that hadn't been a mouse—maybe it had been the ghost of a mouse. The ghost of Jeremiah Bullfrog! If a mouse can scare an elephant, then the ghost of a mouse might scare the ghost of an elephant.

The time had come for Salim to tell the Copycats about Baby Tusker.

10. Salim's Hunch

When Salim got home, he made phone calls to his new friends. "The evening is the best time to talk about ghosts," he said. "Come around to the Mango Tree and I'll tell you what I suspect."

Salim's family lived in a converted barn. In the front room of the house, Salim's dad ran a little shop and takeout restaurant called the Mango Tree. He sold eight kinds of curry that came in the same little square paper boxes. "Very very curried curry," said Mr. Bannerjee, who was always chewing a fragrant mouthful of seeds and sweets together. The shop had brass bangles and temple bells and fabric elephants. Classical Indian ragas wailed prettily from the tape deck. Sticks of incense burned in front of statues, and the lights were turned low. It was the most exotic place between Boston and Montreal. Everybody said so.

The boys trooped upstairs to Salim's bedroom. Sammy Grubb said, "This meeting of the Copycats will come to order. Salim, you said you had a hunch what the ghost was the ghost *of.* Tell us. Was it the six lost hairdressers on the fall foliage tour?"

Salim said, "First, let me share with you a little bit about India."

"Oh no, we don't want to hear about that," groaned Mike. "What do you think this is, public television?"

"Let Salim speak," said Sammy Grubb.

They were sitting on the floor of Salim's room. Salim had hung a red scarf over the lamp to make the room spooky and rosy warm. "My dad was born in Bengal and my mom was born in Bombay," he told them. "They didn't know each other in India. They met when my dad was a student at the Massachusetts Institute of Technology and my mom was at Radcliffe. My dad is Hindu and my mom is Muslim. So I have a very complicated religious life."

The boys waited for this story to start to make sense.

"They got married and had me and my twin baby sisters, Meena and Meera," said Salim. "So I got to go to mosque on Friday nights, and we went to temple other nights. We celebrate both the Hindu and the Muslim holy days. We're always celebrating. It's one of the best things about being Indian."

"Yes?" prompted Sammy patiently.

"Well," said Salim, "sometimes we used to go to a temple in Bombay. It was a temple to honor the deity with the elephant head, Ganesha. Look." He drew aside a couple of scarves he had knotted up into a sort of curtain hanging from his desk drawer.

Underneath his desk, in a little grotto made of desk legs and the edge of his bed, was a brass statue. It was lit by a white candle in a dish. "This is a statue of Ganesha," said Salim, "Sri Ganesha, the elephant god."

"Boy," said Forest Eugene Mopp, whose mother was the Congregationalist minister, "they'd have a stroke if you put anything like this in the First Congregational Church of Hamlet."

The Copycats leaned in to take a closer look. Ganesha was a creature with the legs and torso and arms of a man—and the head of an elephant. He stood on one well-formed foot, muscular calves and thighs rounded in the light. The other foot was arched out, as if he were kicking a football. He had four arms, each holding a complicated brass object. He wore belts and chains and a cap with a little conical point like the top of a baby's first crayon. His stomach swelled in a way that could only be called roly-poly. His ankles and wrists were all ringed with bracelets.

But it was his elephant head that was most wonderful. It was cocked to one side in a joyous way. The trunk snaked around; the ears looked wide and capable, as if they could hear anything in the world. The small eyes, though brass like the rest of him, seemed in their focused way to be kindly.

"There are many divine figures in the Hindu religion," said Salim, "and this one is my favorite. Ganesha, the elephant god. I used to go to his temple in Bombay. Before I left India I made an offering and prayed to have a happy life in Vermont, the United States of America. I was scared that I wouldn't like it and that I would miss my friends."

The other boys had never thought of that. "*Do* you like it here in America?" asked Stanislaus.

"Sure," said Salim firmly.

"Do you like us?" asked Moshe.

"Absolutely," said Salim.

"Do you miss your old friends?" asked Hector.

"Of course I do," said Salim, shocked at the question. "What kind of a person would I be if I didn't?"

"So what are you saying here," said Sammy Grubb, "that some ghostly form of Ganesha has followed you here to Hamlet, Vermont?"

"I don't know," said Salim, "because it's so hard to be sure. But don't you think what we've seen is something like an elephant?" He didn't want to tell them about Baby Tusker yet. He still was ashamed of his part in the elephant's final ailment.

They all thought back. *Could* it have been the ghost of an elephant that showed up in the back yard of Hector Yellow's house? Yes, definitely. And the thing that had been reflected in the water at the quarry pond? Yes, yes. It might just be an elephant. And after all—it had been scared away from Hector's house by Jeremiah Bullfrog, the brown mouse. Elephants were supposed to be scared of mice. What more proof could you need?

"But what does the elephant ghost want from you?" asked Mike.

"I'm not sure," said Salim.

"Why would it try to get into my house?" asked Hector.

"I was there too, remember," said Salim. "But before we figure out what we can do, let's run one more test to make sure my hunch is right."

Salim told the Copycats about the feast of Holi. "That's the time we celebrate the spring harvest. We purify ourselves first. Then we reach for our Holi powder. It's pink and yellow and it comes in packets. It's sort of like talcum powder, only a little gritty. All the shops carry it at the right time of year. We run through the neighborhood and we mark our friends and families with this powder. Or sometimes we dissolve it in tubs and splash colored water on people. It's all in fun; everybody does it. I bet if we got some water guns and mixed up some Holi powder, the next time we saw the ghost we could spray it. Maybe we could fill in the blanks. If you know what I mean."

"Boy, I've heard about pink elephants before," said Sammy, laughing, "but I never thought I'd get a chance to see one! Salim, you're a genius! Let's try it!"

"I only have one problem," said Mike Saint Michael. "Maybe a mouse would terrify a baby elephant ghost. That sort of makes sense. But maybe a mouse would also frighten six lost ladies on a fall foliage tour. We can't be sure this is an elephant ghost yet."

II.
The Six Haunted Hairdos

On the playground during lunch on Monday, Thekla Mustard set the trap. "Any of you boys want to go with me up to the swimming hole by the old quarry after school?" she said to the Copycats. "Maybe we'll be lucky and catch a glimpse of those six lost ladies from the fall foliage tour."

Sammy Grubb could only think of the horrible thing that had lumbered up to Hector's house. He searched for a good excuse. "Oh," he told Thekla, "I read in this morning's Hamlet *Holler* that today's the last day the men are going to be dynamiting for marble on Hardscrabble Hill. Might be dangerous to go wandering around up there. Maybe another time."

"On the other hand," said Thekla cleverly, "it might be fun to see if all that booming noise attracts those six lost ladies from the fall foliage tour."

Thekla was pleased to see the seven Copycats looking antsy.

"I thought boys were brave," Thekla continued. She turned to the girls. "I believe the boys aren't scared of loud noises. They're scared of *ghosts*. Any girls want to come?"

"We don't believe in ghosts; why bother?" said Carly. Nina, Lois, Sharday, Anna Maria, and Fawn nodded in agreement. They went to play jump rope as if to prove the point. As they jumped, they chanted:

Seven sissies never dared
To hunt for ghosts 'cause they were scared.
They saw a sight that made them sicken,
'Cause they're really chick-chick-chicken.
How many phantoms did they see?
One clucka-clucka,
two clucka-clucka,
three clucka-clucka . . .

Pearl Hotchkiss was nearby, throwing a tennis ball up and down. Even though Pearl didn't want to join the Copycats, she had a soft spot in her heart for Sammy Grubb. And she didn't like hearing anyone get teased, boy or girl. "The boys aren't chicken," she said.

"It appears they are," said Thekla. "No one wants to join me for a walk on Hardscrabble Hill. Not that I believe in ghosts, of course; I just feel like a little healthful exercise. But I thought I'd have some brave ghost-hunter boys to join me. Guess they're not brave enough."

"Sammy, do you really think we should—" began Salim, but Sammy Grubb made a sign with his hand that meant: The less said, the better.

"We'll go with you," said Sammy Grubb. "Then we'll see who believes in ghosts."

"Fine," said Thekla. "Let's meet at Grandma's Baked Goods and Auto Repair Shop fifteen minutes after school."

"We'll be there," said Sammy Grubb.

"I'll come too," Pearl Hotchkiss said.

Just then Mrs. Brill, the lunch lady, rang the bell. The kids whizzed around to line up. All of them except Thekla Mustard and Pearl Hotchkiss. The two were in the middle of a heated discussion.

Thekla Mustard was in high gear. She shook her forefinger at Pearl and said, "It's bad enough that you don't want to join the Tattletales. You always say you're an individual. So why are you siding with the boys?"

Pearl was annoyed. "For one thing, Thekla Mustard, it's none of your beeswax. I know you are the Empress of the Tattletales. But you have a mean streak, Thekla, and you bring out the nasty side of them. If I were a Tattletale, I'd vote for someone else for Empress."

"You should join," said Thekla cleverly, "and then nominate yourself."

"I have no interest in joining a club," said Pearl.

"Then why are you siding with the Copycats?" snapped Thekla.

"I'm not siding with the Copycats," said Pearl, "I

just happen to agree with them. I happen to think that ghosts exist. And furthermore, Your Excellency Thekla Mustard, I happen to think that you're up to something. And I'm going to find out what."

Before Thekla could think of a snappy retort, Mrs. Brill was standing between the two girls ringing her bell like a crazy person. "What's wrong, you girls deaf? When I ring to line up, that means line up."

"Sorry, Mrs. Brill," said Pearl. She ran to get in line.

"Mrs. Brill," said Thekla Mustard, "urgent matters required my attention. This in no way undermines your very important position of authority as lunch lady at the Josiah Fawcett Elementary School. Furthermore, may I add—"

"You may not," said Mrs. Brill. "Who died and made you grand queen poobah? Get in line and save your breath."

Thekla walked across the playground and got in line with as much dignity as she could muster, given that most of the other kids were laughing at her. She didn't care. She was starting to worry about how much Pearl Hotchkiss knew. Pearl was smart. If she was siding with the Copycats, the Tattletales would have to watch their step.

After school while the Tattletales raced to Fawn's house to get dressed in their costumes, Thekla dragged her feet on purpose and was late getting to Grandma Earth's shop. "Sorry, school chums," she said when she arrived. "I had to return some books to the library."

The Copycats and Pearl were almost done with their after-school doughnuts when an ear-splitting *boom* sledgehammered the sky.

"Time we were going, I guess," said Thekla. "Good-bye, Grandma Earth."

"Now if you see anything unusual, let me know," said Grandma Earth. "I haven't heard anything about this minivan crash into the swimming hole. I'll ask about it on the CB radio and see if anyone can tell us more."

The Copycats and Pearl Hotchkiss and Thekla Mustard walked along Squished Toad Road, then turned off through the meadows of Old Man Fingerpie's farm. Beyond the farm the gentle curves of Hardscrabble Hill began, and it was a bit of a hike. The children paused for breath halfway up.

"Of course, it was a terrible tragedy," said Thekla Mustard. "I mean when the minivan went pitching into the swimming hole. I understand the driver was on TV a few weeks ago. He was talking about it to Meg Snoople, the famous talk-show reporter. He told her that the six lost ladies had been singing at the top of their lungs when the minivan went around the bend and tumbled through the air into the swimming hole."

"What were they singing?" asked Sammy Grubb.

"I thought it might be 'Ninety-Nine Bottles of Beer on the Wall.' You know those fall foliage tours. They get pretty zany," said Thekla Mustard. "But the driver said they were all singing 'Stick with Your Man,' that number one country-and-western hit made famous by Petunia Whiner."

"Any idea who the ladies were?" asked Stan.

"The minivan driver said that they were six part-time hairdressers. They all worked at the same salon in a shopping mall in Massachusetts somewhere. Monday through Saturday, each one had a day. But they were all different. When they weren't doing hairdressing, they had other things to do. One was a sheep farmer. One was a lounge singer. One was a nun. One was a trash collector. One looked like Dorothy in *The Wizard of Oz*. And one was a fisher-woman."

"How can you remember all that?" said Pearl Hotchkiss. "Sounds fishy to me."

"I have a sharp mind," said Thekla tartly. "Human nature interests me. Not ghost nature."

"Well, whatever happens, let's all stay together," said Sammy Grubb. "Agreed?"

"Agreed," said Thekla. Sammy was surprised. Thekla was not usually so agreeable.

"Come on, let's go," said Pearl. "We need to get up and back before it gets dark."

"Oh, oh, I twisted my ankle!" said Thekla suddenly, pretending to stumble, and tumbling onto the ground. "I'm such a weak little girlish thing, full of sugar and spice and everything nice! The pain is almost unbearable! Fie!"

"Fie?" said Pearl.

"*Fie* is an old-fashioned expression that, roughly

speaking, can be translated as *phooey*," said Thekla. "What ever shall we do?"

"I guess we better turn back," said Sammy Grubb. The boys nodded enthusiastically.

Another *boom* thundered through the air.

"I wouldn't hear of it!" said Thekla. "I'll hobble bravely on! That is, if you boys would let me lean on your strong shoulders." Normally Thekla wouldn't be caught dead saying such namby-pamby things. Normally the boys wouldn't be caught dead letting Thekla Mustard lean on them. But the Copycats felt trapped in the turn of events. And Thekla enjoyed the excuse of a fake broken ankle to pretend to be even more helpless and useless. Make the boys seem even braver and stronger by comparison—and then she could laugh all the heartier at their cowardice and fright when the Six Haunted Hairdos scared them!

"I don't like the look of this," Salim muttered to Sammy Grubb. "It's already getting darkish."

"This is New England in November. It gets dark early," said Sammy. "Don't worry."

They continued along the path up Hardscrabble Hill. The winds picked up. The skies turned a sort of purple brown. The rumbling of heavy machinery could be heard from the other side of the hill several miles away.

"Pretty soon it will get too cold to do this sort of quarrying," said Pearl to Salim, "so they'll stop for the winter."

"I never in my life saw it get so cold," said Salim.

"Maybe that's why these lost ladies from the fall foliage tour are being sighted now," said Thekla, improvising. "Maybe they don't want to be frozen ghosts in the swimming hole all winter long."

"Thekla, we better turn back," said Sammy. "With your bad ankle, it'll be fully dark by the time we get up there and back."

"Why, Sammy Grubb, I do believe you're scared," said Thekla. "Are you wimping out on me? I thought boys were supposed to be the brave ones."

"I'm just being sensible," said Sammy.

"That's what you say," said Thekla. "I'm all for going on. Who's with me on this?"

Pearl was determined that Thekla wouldn't get away with anything. Pearl raised her hand. "On we go, then, Pearl, with or without the sensitive boys," said Thekla firmly.

So on they all continued, because how could the boys back down now?

By the time they drew near the swimming hole, dusk was upon them. The booms seemed to have finished for the day. The raw and gloomy woods around the swimming hole were thick with violet shadows. The children could barely see to the other side of the water. It was hard to focus. Their voices dropped.

"Baby Tusker, stay away," mumbled Salim.

"Oh dear, I *am* worried," said Thekla. "I thought I wouldn't be spooked but I am. Silly me."

Suddenly a creepy kind of country-and-western music drifted from the other side of the water.

"What is that?" hissed Pearl.

"Everybody be very careful," whispered Salim.

"I feel the hairs on my arms standing up," said Sammy Grubb.

"I feel sweat running down my armpits," said Mike Saint Michael.

"I feel my mouth going dry," said Stan Tomaski.

"I feel my knees knocking like castanets," said Hector Yellow.

"I feel my teeth chattering like nobody's business," said Moshe Cohn.

"I feel like going home," said Forest Eugene Mopp.

"I feel cold," said Salim Bannerjee.

"I feel stupid," said Pearl Hotchkiss. "Let's get outa here."

"Wait!" whispered Thekla. She pointed a finger across the pond. "Look!"

"What is it?" cried Sammy Grubb.

"Six Haunted Hairdos!" announced Thekla Mustard.

And there they came, snaking through the trees, doing a little sort of slow-motion dance on the far side of the swimming hole. Six ghostly apparitions: Fawn the Inflammable Fleece, Lois the Lounge Singer, Sister Anna Maria Spokehead, Carly the Trash Collector, Shar-Dorothay, and Nina the Queen of the Marine Scene. They were festooned in veils of flimsy gauze, from the tips of their wigs right down to their ankles. In their huge hairdos, they looked like clipped hedges wandering about the forest. The special effects were spectacular.

"Eat your heart out, Steven Spielberg!" muttered Thekla Mustard proudly. She couldn't help herself.

The lost ladies, the Six Haunted Hairdos, the Tattletales. They were magnificent! As if sleepwalking, they held their arms straight ahead and marched in slow motion, glancing neither left nor right, disappearing behind trees and reappearing again. Their reflections in the dark water were even creepier than they were. It almost looked as if they were walking upside down in the perfectly still water, trying to find a way out.

"Everybody steady," said Sammy Grubb. "Don't lose your nerve."

Suddenly an unexpected *boom* slammed through the air. The boys all fell to the ground. Even Thekla Mustard pitched herself earthward and forgot she was supposed to have a broken ankle. Before they knew it, Thekla and Pearl and the Copycats were racing down Hardscrabble Hill, screaming for their lives. By the time they got to the bottom, it was completely dark.

"Thekla, your ankle," said Sammy Grubb, when he could catch his breath.

"I think that noise jostled the bone back into place, because it feels just fine now," said Thekla.

"So now do you believe in ghosts?" asked Sammy. "You saw them as clearly as we did!"

"Saw what?" said Thekla innocently.

"The Six Haunted Hairdos!" cried Sammy.

"I'm not sure I actually *saw* anything," said Thekla. "Perhaps those were just shadows in the woods. Or maybe trees and branches shifting in the wind and reflecting in the water. I can't be sure I saw Six Haunted Hairdos."

"You saw what we saw!" shouted Hector. "How can you say that?"

"I keep my own counsel," said Thekla Mustard sweetly. "We'll talk about it in school tomorrow. Ta ta, fellows." She went sprinting to home.

"Well, *I* saw them," said Pearl Hotchkiss. She hugged herself and rubbed her arms to get warm. "I just wonder how Thekla's ankle got better all of a sudden."

But Salim was thinking: I guess that wasn't the ghost of Baby Tusker. He was partly relieved and—though he was surprised at this—he was partly sorry, too.

12

The Triumph of the Tattletales

When Miss Earth called her students to order the next day, the chatting didn't die down. If anything, it got more chattery.

"Class," said Miss Earth. "Come to order, please."

Sammy Grubb stood and shook his fist at Thekla Mustard. Thekla Mustard stood and stuck out her tongue at Sammy Grubb.

"Class," said Miss Earth. "If you would kindly postpone this heated chat."

The Copycats were turning red and white. The Tattletales were turning white and red. Pearl Hotchkiss took this opportunity to think about Sammy Grubb and how much she liked him, so she could blush as much as she wanted and nobody would notice.

"Class," said Miss Earth, "I hate to interrupt such enthusiastic conversation, but I am forced to say: *Will you clam up!*"

The class shut up at once. Miss Earth so seldom raised her voice that they were astonished.

"Would one of you please tell me what is going on?" said Miss Earth.

Thekla Mustard sprang to her feet. "Dear Miss Earth," she said, "the boys and Pearl Hotchkiss claim to have seen ghosts yesterday up on Hardscrabble Hill! Did you ever hear of anything so ridiculous? I wonder if they'll see little fairies under the tulips next spring! Or the Easter Bunny lolloping along, hiding eggs!"

"I never saw the Easter Bunny, but I always look," said Fawn under her breath.

Miss Earth said, "Would one of the boys care to explain what all this is about?"

Sammy Grubb was too furious to get any words out. Salim nibbled a fingernail. Hector's jaw was open. Stan's was clamped shut. Forest Eugene shook his head in dismay. Moshe was hiding his face in his hands. Mike was pretending to tie his shoe. The boys were just too embarrassed to speak.

Pearl Hotchkiss raised her hand. When Miss Earth nodded at her to speak, she stood and said, "Miss Earth, I was there too. I saw the ghosts of six hairdressers. Thekla called them the Six Haunted Hairdos, and that's what they looked like. They looked like beauticians gone berserk. The ghosts were frightening, and they were *there*. We came, we saw, we crumpled. If Thekla doesn't admit it, she's either lying to herself or to us. Why did you run screaming down the hill, Thekla, if you weren't scared of something?

And funny how your wounded ankle suddenly healed itself, by the way."

"I saw a flurry of leaves; I heard the wind in the trees," said Thekla calmly. "Then there was that last blast of dynamite from the quarry on the other side of Hardscrabble Hill. It startled me. The blast probably jolted my bone back into its proper place. So I ran to keep everyone else company. I make no apologies for my strong community feeling."

"It's eight to one," said Pearl. "Eight of us saw the Six Haunted Hairdos. One of us pretends she didn't see them. I don't think there's any reason to keep talking about it. *Ghosts exist.* Now we have proof."

Pearl sat down. The Copycats were grateful for her support. Sammy Grubb flashed her the briefest of smiles.

Pearl was never sure what Sammy Grubb thought of her, so now she felt as if life was suddenly more wonderful than it had been an instant before.

"Well," said Miss Earth, "I think the school board would not be pleased if we spent the rest of the month arguing about ghosts. But I am here to promote an air of inquiry. Do you have theories about what you saw yesterday?"

"I believe," said Thekla Mustard, "that something in Grandma Earth's doughnuts provoked a moment of mass hysteria. A communal swoon, if you will. Not uncommon among simple-minded boys."

"I believe," said Sammy Grubb, regaining his composure, "that we saw the ghosts of six dead hairdressers. May they rest in peace."

"I think," said Pearl Hotchkiss, "that there's more to this than meets the eye. But I don't know what and I don't want to say."

"None of the other girls have spoken," said Miss Earth. "Carly? Anna Maria? Sharday? Fawn? Lois? Nina?"

The Tattletales shook their heads and bit their lips and blinked their eyes a lot. Fawn flipped her thick stack of hair into her face and her shoulders shook with silent laughter.

"Well then," said Miss Earth, "we'll have to postpone discussion until someone has further evidence of these supposed phantoms. But let me remind you of what one of my favorite country-and-western songs says." She hummed a note to herself to make sure her pitch was perfect—not much chance of that, alas—and began:

It's quarter to midnight and what should I do?
I'm haunted by even the memory of you.
There are phantoms abroad when the stars shine above.
In the dark I meet up with the ghost of our love.

The class clapped politely.

"By this I mean," said Miss Earth, "if there are such things as ghosts, surely love would be the strongest reason for them to remain. Isn't love the strongest reason for everything?"

Miss Earth had never looked so beautiful or mysterious. Pearl found herself wondering if Miss Earth was in love. It would have to be some sort of grown-up version of Sammy Grubb. Pearl smiled to herself. The smile seemed too good to waste, so then she smiled at Sammy Grubb. But he was too busy biting his fingernails to notice. Those Haunted Hairdos had really spooked him. What could Pearl do to help?

13
The Cohoes Mastodon

For the rest of the week the girls lorded it over the boys. "I smell a rat," said Pearl Hotchkiss, over and over again. For one thing, there was that ankle suddenly healing itself. But though Pearl lingered on the edges of the Tattletales' jump-rope competitions and even joined in, she could pick up no clue as to what was going on.

Then the weekend came. Stanislaus Tomaski and his mother and her friend Tish all piled into the car and headed toward New York State. Mr. and Mrs. Tomaski were divorced, but his mom drove Stan once a month to Cohoes, New York, where his dad lived. Mrs. Tomaski and Tish usually hung around until the end of the weekend, when they picked Stan up and drove home to Hamlet, Vermont.

Mr. Tomaski worked in a hardware store. Sometimes on Saturday mornings he had to put in extra hours. When this happened, Stan read the comics in the newspaper and he listened to his dad's collection of vintage rock-and-roll. However, this weekend Stan was so interested in ghosts that he asked his dad for his library card. Mr. Tomaski said sure and handed it over. "You know where the library is, Stanislaus, we pass it all the time on the way to the store. It's in that converted church."

So Stan made his way to the Cohoes Public Library. It was a week before Thanksgiving, and the stores all had cardboard pilgrims and turkeys in their windows. It was an overcast Saturday morning, and lots of little kids were out scribbling on the sidewalks with chalk. It made Stan feel grown-up to walk to a library he didn't even know, through knots and clots of tiny kids playing.

But when he got to the library, and his eyes adjusted to the gloom, he thought he was having hallucinations. He thought the ghost elephant had followed him from Vermont.

"This is crazy," he whispered.

Then he saw a sheet of Plexiglas in front of the vision, and he realized that ghosts don't travel around with their own bulletproof Plexiglas shields. Some-thing stood behind the Plexiglas, on what must have been the old altar of the church before it was desanctified. It was a life-size model of a shaggy elephant. Balefully it stared, with enormous tusks and a trunk like a fire hose.

"What *is* this?" said Stan. He went up to the librarian. "Please, Ms. Librarian. What is that thing over there?"

"That's the famous stuffed model of the Cohoes

Mastodon," said the librarian quietly. An old man reading a newspaper glared at her and said, "Shhhh!" She made a face at him behind his back and kept on talking to Stan. "There was a skeleton of a mastodon dug up in Cohoes, a long time ago. This is an artist's reconstruction of what a mastodon might have looked like, back in the days before they became extinct, like dinosaurs."

"It's the best thing I ever saw," said Stan.

"Me, too, even though scientists now question how accurate this model is. Knowledge marches on, or pretends to, anyway. But I have a special fondness for it. So do most kids."

"It's so . . . hairy," said Stan.

"It's not quite the same thing as a woolly mammoth, but that's what it makes me think of," said the librarian. "Mastodons died out about eight thousand years ago, but there were still woolly mammoths around as recently as three or four thousand years ago."

"Shhh!" said the old man.

"Shhh yourself!" said the librarian, Stan, and twelve other patrons. The man hid behind his newspaper.

"I wonder if mastodons or woolly mammoths ever lived in Vermont." said Stan.

"Wouldn't be surprised," said the librarian. "Southern Vermont isn't more than fifty or sixty miles from here."

"Thanks a lot," said Stan. "You've been loads of help."

He went up and looked at the thing, as close as he could get. He imagined he saw it move. He thought he could see its foot just about to lift off the platform.

"It doesn't move," said the old man on his way out. "You keep staring as if you think it's going to move. It doesn't move. This isn't Disneyland, you know. This is a library."

"I know where there's one that does move," said Stan, not meanly, just honestly.

"Yeah sure," said the old man. "And they say that the elderly are the ones who lose their marbles." He went out.

Not *all* old people are wonderful, Stanislaus thought. I sure wouldn't like to be haunted by *him*. Stan looked admiringly at the mastodon some more. Much better to be haunted by *you*, or some distant cousin of yours.

14
The Ghostdusters

The very same Saturday that Stanislaus Tomaski was enraptured by the mastodon in Cohoes, New York, Pearl Hotchkiss made her own trip to the library in Hamlet, Vermont.

Mr. Dewey was a nice librarian. He had little scraps of hair on the top of his head like the down that seeps out of a sleeping bag. Graying hair sproinged at his temples. He wore striped shirts with old fashioned metal bracelet-type things on his forearms to keep his shirtsleeves up. He smelled as if he ate sandwiches made out of library paste—a rather agreeable smell. It made Pearl hungry and also eager to read a good book. Mr. Dewey said to Pearl, "Can I help you find anything special this morning?"

"I need to see some back issues of the Hamlet *Holler*," said Pearl.

"What month?" said Mr. Dewey.

"I don't even know what year," said Pearl. "I want to read up on the crash of that minivan into the old swimming hole up on Hardscrabble Hill."

"I don't remember anything about that," said Mr. Dewey, looking through his bifocals kindly at Pearl. "Where'd you come across that story?"

"Everybody knows about it," said Pearl. "Six hairdressers from a salon called Curl Up and Dye down in Massachusetts went to their watery grave singing 'Stick with Your Man.' Their bodies were never recovered. It was a fall foliage tour that ended in senseless tragedy for all except the minivan driver, who lived to tell the tale." She concluded strongly, "Now the Six Haunted Hairdos, as they're called, are stalking Hamlet. Ghosts on the loose. I saw them myself."

"Oh, you did?" said Mr. Dewey. "Where?"

"Up on Hardscrabble Hill. Please, can you help? Maybe we could find something on the driver who survived."

"I think I'd remember about that," said Mr. Dewey. "I've been the librarian here for twelve years. But let's look it up in the *All-Vermont Road Injury Index*. The index is updated every six months. They've got a section for animal roadkill and another one for damage to human beings. Surely we'll find something there."

The *All-Vermont Road Injury Index* was a slim paperback book about the size of a folded-up state map. The only listing under "Hamlet, Vermont" was the truck crash in early September, when a Mr. Pierre Montrose had overturned his vehicle on Route 89 and seven Siberian snow spiders had escaped into the woods.

"I don't understand this," said Pearl. "Something is fishy here."

"I can't help you much, I'm afraid," said Mr. Dewey. "The thing that puzzles me is this: How did the minivan get up to the swimming hole anyway? At least as far as I remember from when I used to go swimming, there's no road going up there."

"There's a cut-through logging road that the men in the quarry use," said Pearl.

"That old road is completely overgrown now," said Mr. Dewey. "Think about it. The swimming hole is in the old quarry that's been mined out since the 1940s. The new quarry, the one they blast in, is on the other side of Hardscrabble Hill, and the access road comes up from behind the high school. If there really were a terrible minivan accident in the swimming hole, it could only have happened fifty years ago when the road to the swimming hole wasn't so overgrown."

"Well, maybe it did," said Pearl.

"But," said Mr. Dewey, "fifty years ago, minivans hadn't been invented yet."

"Aha!" cried Pearl. "I knew I smelled a rat! Thanks, Mr. Dewey!"

"Might I interest you in this copy of *Alfred Hitchcock's Ghostly Gallery*?" said Mr. Dewey, pulling a book from the shelf.

"Thanks," said Pearl and took it to be polite. But she raced on her bike over to Sammy Grubb's house. She was so pleased to have a reason to go there! Sammy seemed a little surprised to see her, but he was glad to hear what she had learned.

"Pearl," he said, "your parents named you well. You *are* a pearl."

Pearl wanted to say something equally wonderful back, but saying "And you're a grub" didn't have the same smack. So she just grinned and dropped her biking helmet on her foot.

Was this love, or just a nice strong sort of liking? She didn't know.

Sammy invited Pearl to stay for an emergency meeting of the Copycats. Then he got on the phone and told everyone to meet in the Ethan Allen Park and to come prepared for Operation Ghostduster. All the Copycats were there except for Stan, who was still in New York visiting his father. The boys were incensed when they learned that there was no such thing as a minivan crash of beauticians into the old swimming hole.

"Then what did we see?" said Forest Eugene Mopp.

"It wasn't any elephant, that's for sure," said Salim. "But maybe there is another ghost lurking about. It's possible. Look, I brought some peanuts with me. Didn't the ghost in Old Man Fingerpie's house pick up the peanuts out of Pearl's sack on Halloween? I have an idea."

Salim was still sensitive about Baby Tusker. But he figured that a ghost that had already died of an evil stomach virus brought on by an overdose of peanuts couldn't die again. There was no such thing as the ghost of a ghost, was there?

"So what are we going to do now?" asked Pearl.

"Well," said Sammy, "we're going to go back up on Hardscrabble Hill and hunt for the ghost. See, the thing I figure is this. Look at the places we've sighted the ghost. One: the old swimming hole near the quarry. Two: Hector Yellow's back yard. Three: Old Man Fingerpie's farmhouse. What do these three places have in common?"

"The old swimming hole's on Hardscrabble Hill," said Forest Eugene.

"My house backs up on Hardscrabble Hill," said Hector.

"So does Old Man Fingerpie's farm," said Mike.

"Exactly," said Sammy Grubb. "Whatever the Six Haunted Hairdos may or may not be, I think Hardscrabble Hill is the ghost's stomping ground. So our plan today is to lure the ghost out and dust it with pink Holi powder."

"What is Holi powder?" asked Pearl.

"Holi powder and pink water," said Salim, pulling a plastic bucket out of his knapsack. Inside were a dozen small plastic satchels of a flourlike substance. From their backpacks the boys were taking an impressive artillery of water guns. Using the public fountain in the park, Salim mixed up some pink water in his bucket, and the boys loaded their ammunition.

"We'll have to stick together," said Salim. "One of us can climb a tree. If the others can lure the ghost underneath, the tree climber can shower the top of it with handfuls of this powder. If my hunch is correct, the powder will stick to the ghost's outline, the way leaves seemed to. Like iron filings around a magnet. Like Shake 'N Bake breading on chicken. The rest of us can color in the sides. At least we'll get a good view of what we're dealing with. And maybe that'll give us a suggestion what to do next."

They headed up the edges of Hardscrabble Hill, where it rose bleak and gray from the far corner of Ethan Allen Park. The trees were close to leafless by now. The tree trunks made a vertical pattern of gray and black stripes against the brown carpet of leaves on the slope. It felt spooky.

As Chief of the Copycats, Sammy Grubb conferred closely with Salim, who in this operation was second in command. They decided that they would spread out. Mike and Hector would start at Hector's house and work in. Moshe and Forest Eugene would work down from the quarry pool. Sammy and Salim would come up from Old Man Fingerpie's farm. Pearl would wait in a tree. If the ghost was around they would corner it. "The middle location, I think, is that grove of oak trees near Smugglers' Lookout," said Sammy.

"Fine," said Pearl. "But how can I be sure you can flush the ghost close enough for me to dust the top of it with fistfuls of this stuff?"

"That's where the peanuts come in," said Salim. "Here, everybody, take these bags of nuts. Spread them on the ground underneath the tree Pearl is in. With luck it may attract our ghostly friend."

"Operation Ghostduster is about to begin," said Sammy Grubb. "Everyone ready? Any last words?"

"Should we sing something?" said Pearl. "I mean

just in case one of us gets wounded in the line of duty or something?"

The boys snorted but Salim liked the idea. "Puts us in the right spirit," he said. "Good spirits are very important in dealing with spirits. Any suggestions?"

In the end, and despite the fact that she wasn't there, they sang another one of Miss Earth's favorite country-and-western songs, the one that went, "You lie, you steal, and did I mention, / You'd cheat your mama of her old-age pension." It wasn't appropriate but it did draw their anxious hearts together as all good music must.

Then without further ado they split up.

Pearl made her way to the oak trees around Smugglers' Lookout. This was a forested bluff that commanded a good view up and down the valley. When Pearl had settled comfortably in the generous boughs of the oak tree, she could see the spire of the First Congregational Church of Hamlet, the local supermarket, the library, the general store, the school, and a lot of private homes, thinning out as they got farther from the center of the village.

It felt as if she waited for hours. But finally there was a thrashing sound nearby. Pearl put her hands into the plastic sack and readied a handful of pink powder. She could just make out Sammy and Salim, who were about fifty feet away and moving slowly through the underbrush with their water guns at chest level. "Here we come, slow but sure," sang out Sammy in a high voice. "We might have to circle back, but we'll get it sooner or later!"

A short time later there was the sound of boys from the other sides of the clearing, and the thrashing and crashing grew more pronounced.

"Unless it pitches itself off the cliff, it'll be forced in here," Pearl said. She was so nervous she was talking to herself. "And what ghost wants to commit suicide? I mean, what would be the point? It's already dead."

Suddenly there was a stirring of leaves on the ground underneath her. The brown oak leaves, crisp and crackling, whirred around. The limbs in the trees began to sway, though there was no wind. "Ready?" called Sammy.

"Ready," said Pearl.

"Aim," said Sammy.

"Aim," said Pearl to herself.

"Fire," said Sammy in a conversational tone.

"Fire," said Pearl. She let fistfuls of Holi powder sail through the air.

The ghostdusting was working! A shape was emerging in the grove of oak trees at the edge of Smugglers' Lookout. Something huge, with a backbone like the ridgepole of a roof. It was eleven or twelve feet high. At first it looked like a hanging sheet in the air, a pink tablecloth spread unevenly out. Then the boys opened fire from ground level and sprayed the lower section of the ghost with their high-powered water guns.

Pinkly the ghost emerged out of the chestnut and charcoal colors of the forest. It was as Salim had guessed. It was an elephant, a huge odd creature, with smudgy edges. As if it guessed it had become visible, it stopped and lowered its head. Its trunk went foraging along the forest floor and found a peanut. It picked it up and sniffed it.

The boys inched slowly forward.

"Look," said Salim. "I think it's crying."

15
Salim's Secret

The ghost shifted forward. It stood among them for a while, or sort of stood; its big tree-trunk legs wavered in the breeze, like smoke rising from a campfire.

"Nobody move," Salim said. "The ghost seems friendly enough but elephants don't like fast movements." But Salim looked a little gray. *Was* it the ghost of Baby Tusker? It was mighty big for a baby elephant. Ghosts didn't keep growing after they died, did they?

Pearl came down from the tree, carefully, and joined the boys. The kids stood around the apparition like a Ghost Elephant Support Group, almost close enough to touch its wisping, misty pink sides. "It isn't really eating those peanuts," whispered Moshe Cohn. "It's just picking them up and putting them down again."

Then—to everyone's surprise—there was a *boom*. But it wasn't a dynamite explosion from the other side of Hardscrabble Hill; it was a jet crossing the sound barrier, high up in the sky. The ghost elephant seemed agitated by the boom. Its ears began to flap, dislodging puffs of Holi powder into the air. Its eyes streamed with elephant tears, which rolled up into little balls of clotted pink powder as they dropped to the ground. It raised its trunk and made an answering sound—a sort of ghost elephant snort—and it began to lumber up the hill.

"Should we follow it?" whispered Pearl.

"No," Salim said. "Elephants are like small kids. They learn to trust you a little at a time. We don't want it to think we're chasing it. However, if we get some more peanuts and leave them here, maybe it'll come back."

They watched the elephant disappear through the forest, like a lumbering cloud. It was hard to say how long the Holi powder would stick to it. But when the ghost had gone, Sammy Grubb turned and saw that Salim had tears in his eyes.

"Are you feeling homesick for India?" said Sammy.

"No," said Salim. "But I guess I better confess my awful crime. Maybe you won't want me to be a Copycat anymore."

"Let's go up to the tree house," said Sammy. "We can get some Doritos to fortify us and you can tell us then. Pearl, you're invited if you want to come."

"Sammy!" said Moshe, Hector, Mike, and Forest Eugene, all at the same time. They sounded horrified.

"The Copycats is a club for boys and only boys," said Mike.

"I'm not asking her to be a member," said Sammy.

"After all, Pearl did witness what we witnessed, *and* she's the only girl in the class who believes in ghosts."

"I wouldn't join the Copycats club if you asked me to," said Pearl pointedly. "I have five sisters and a brother. I don't need to belong to a club. My whole family is a club."

"Pearl could be a valuable secret agent on our behalf, if she chose," said Sammy Grubb. "I am going to insist that we invite her to our meeting, guys."

"You're the Chief," said Salim. The other boys groaned, but shrugged their shoulders.

Sammy Grubb turned back to Pearl and said, "You are welcome if you want to join us."

"Okay," said Pearl. "I don't have anything better to do, anyway." Since she had never been invited to the Copycats' fort before, she was thrilled. But she'd still rather be a guest than a member any day.

They trooped back down Hardscrabble Hill. Nobody said anything until they got to Sammy Grubb's tree house, where they settled on the floorboards and looked at Salim expectantly.

"What I want to know is this," said Sammy Grubb to Salim. "Do you think that this is some sort of elephant guardian angel sent from India to check up on you in Vermont? An agent of that four-armed creature, Ganesha? Come to make sure you're making friends and being happy?"

"I really can't tell," said Salim. "But I have a hunch that it's not."

"Then what do you think it is?" said Sammy.

Salim sighed. He put his face in his hands for a

minute. But then he gathered his courage and began. "Last summer, a couple of weeks before we moved from Bombay, I fed some peanuts to a sick newborn elephant named Baby Tusker. There was a sign asking visitors not to feed the elephant because it was sick, but I didn't see it. The poor elephant's mother had just died of the same ailment. And then Baby Tusker died too. I felt terrible. It was all my fault."

"It wasn't your fault if you didn't see the sign!" cried Pearl.

"But I still did it," said Salim. "If I hadn't fed Baby Tusker, perhaps it would be alive today. So I am afraid that what we saw on Hardscrabble Hill may be the ghost of Baby Tusker, come back to haunt me until the end of my days."

"I have only one problem with this theory," said Sammy Grubb. "That ghost elephant didn't look like any baby to me. It was eleven feet tall."

"The thing is," said Hector Yellow, "if it's a real ghost, it wants something. Ghosts hang around for a purpose. To complete unfinished business. But there's always a way to get them to stop haunting you. Always a way to help them."

Salim said, "But what can I do?"

"What can *we* do, you mean," said Sammy Grubb kindly. "We're all in this together, you know."

Salim smiled in a wobbly way. He was too touched to say any more.

Pearl said, "If what we just saw up at Hardscrabble Hill was a ghost elephant, then who or what did we see singing 'Stick with Your Man' the other day?"

The boys were silent.

"Whatever we saw wasn't a herd of elephants," said Pearl. "I have my own theory about what it was. If I can prove it, I'll come back and let you know."

"You have our permission to sneak around," said Sammy Grubb.

"I don't need your permission to sneak around," said Pearl. "But if you want to know what I find out, you better vote about whether I'm invited back—as a guest, of course. I'm not interested in being a member."

The boys looked doubtful.

"And the vote better be unanimous," said Pearl. "I like to feel wanted, especially when I'm putting myself in danger."

"All in favor of Pearl Hotchkiss being invited back to tell us what she learns," said Sammy Grubb, "hands up."

The hands went up slowly, but the hands did go up. Every one.

"All in favor," reported Sammy Grubb with satisfaction. "Thank you, guys. Pearl, it is our pleasure to invite you back to report on what you find."

"Wish me well," said Pearl Hotchkiss. "I'm going into enemy territory, Copycats." As she disappeared down the rungs of the ladder nailed to the tree trunk, she was whistling "Stick with Your Man."

16
Multiple Ghosts

Pearl knew that the Tattletales often met at Thekla's house. But she also knew that Fawn Petros' mother was the owner of the Hamlet House of Beauty. And everything having to do with hair in Hamlet, Vermont, took place at the Hamlet House of Beauty. So that's where she headed.

Pearl opened the door. The air inside the beauty shop was moist and perfumed and sort of gluey. Mrs. Petros was poised over a blue rinse on Widow Wendell. Widow Wendell had her head tipped backward into a special sink with fancy hoses attached.

"The whole idea of haunted hairdos gives me a shiver," Widow Wendell was saying. "Make sure you put in a creme rinse, Gladys, or the permanent curl comes out during the evening news."

As far as Pearl was concerned, Widow Wendell didn't have enough hair to curl, permanently or otherwise. But Pearl wasn't there to investigate hair trends. "Hi, Mrs. Petros, is Fawn home?" said Pearl.

"She and the gal-pals are upstairs having a hoot and a holler," said Fawn's mother. "Go on up. Door's open." Mrs. Petros turned and plunged her hands into the water, lathering Widow Wendell's head, and continued her conversation. "The whole town is buzzing about haunted hairdos. I want to go on record here and now that my hair fashions are the most up-to-date around. I'll flatten anyone who even hints that any of my handiwork is haunted."

"I wouldn't dream of suggesting it!" cried Widow Wendell, which was smart of her, as Mrs. Petros was well positioned to drown her in the rinsing basin if the need arose.

Interesting as this was, Pearl Hotchkiss had other things on her mind. Up the stairs at the back of the hair salon she tiptoed, right to the door of the apartment where Fawn lived with her mother. Pearl put her ear to the keyhole, glad that nice Mr. Dewey had recommended *Harriet the Spy* to her at the library three weeks ago. Now Pearl knew all about spying.

"Did you see those boys dash?" Pearl recognized Thekla's superior tone in an instant. "Girls, I've already congratulated you on your pizzazz, but let me state again: You were magnificent!"

"When that blast came, we all fell to the ground," said Fawn. "It was lucky we didn't fall into the swimming hole, or we'd be Six Soggy Spooks!"

"Six Damp Damsels," trilled Carly.

"Six Soaking Specters!" suggested Nina.

"Six Wet Wigs!" chortled Sharday.

"Six Teeth-Chattering Tattletales!" said Lois.

"Six Sinking Sisters," cried Anna Maria.

"Six feet under," concluded Thekla, in a less happy voice. "We're lucky tragedy didn't strike. If we ever decide to have another appearance of the Six Haunted Hairdos, girls, we'll have to be more careful. We don't want the boys to come to any harm, but we don't want ourselves to suffer, either."

"Surely we're not going to do it again," said Lois. Pearl could tell that Lois was needling Thekla, trying to undercut Thekla's authority, as usual. "Surely once is enough. The important thing is that our little trick worked. Those boys are scared out of their pants. To scare them again would go beyond funny and start being nasty." There was a mumble of agreement.

The Tattletales didn't want to hate the Copycats. They just wanted to be better than them. Pearl knew that was pretty much how the Copycats felt about the Tattletales, too. What a waste of energy, thought Pearl.

Thekla, ever the adroit leader, didn't argue with Lois. Instead, Thekla began to sing. The other girls took up the chorus.

> *Blizzards snow, tornadoes blow,*
> *Ingrown toenails come and go.*
> *Troubles grow, but even so,*
> *Girl, here's what you gotta know:*
> *Stick with your hair!*

The girls all screamed with laughter at Thekla's new last line. Lois' divisive comment was eclipsed for now. What a genius Thekla Mustard is, thought Pearl.

Pearl went back downstairs and out the door of the shop.

"I'm back," said Pearl, at the base of the tree in Sammy Grubb's back yard.

"Be our guest," called Sammy.

Pearl could almost hear him giving a frown to the other boys to make them be quiet. She climbed up quickly and threw herself down on the boards. "Listen up, guys," she said. "We've been had, in a big way, and by none other than those smart-alecky Tattletales."

"No!" said Sammy. "Say it ain't so!"

"Think about it," said Pearl. "Wasn't it Thekla's idea to go up and look for the Six Haunted Hairdos? The other six Tattletales didn't want to go. So who *did* we see on the other side of the swimming hole? You figure it out."

"How devious," said Salim Bannerjee.

"How diabolical," said Forest Eugene Mopp.

"How cunning," said Mike Saint Michael.

"How clever," said Moshe Cohn.

"How embarrassing," said Hector Yellow.

"How did they do it?" asked Sammy Grubb.

"I'm not sure," said Pearl Hotchkiss. "But we've been made fools of, all of us. The clue was right there. Thekla's sprained ankle that suddenly unsprained itself? A likely story."

"But Hardscrabble Hill is haunted," said Sammy Grubb. "We proved it once and for all."

"Yes, it is haunted," said Pearl. "But by a ghost elephant, *not* by Six Haunted Hairdos."

"This is dreadful," said Sammy Grubb. "I want revenge against those girls."

"Don't talk about revenge," said Salim. "Look what I'm up against—a ghost is haunting me for revenge."

"The elephant ghost we saw isn't out to get you," said Sammy firmly. "The ghost is looking for something, and if we can figure out what that something is, we'll find it. I don't mind doing a good deed for a ghost. But the trick that the Tattletales played on us is a separate issue. It makes me clammy all over just to think about how we've been tricked. How humiliating!"

"Sammy," said Pearl Hotchkiss, "the idea of revenge *is* tempting. But let's postpone our revenge until we figure out how to help that poor ghost elephant. I'm going to go back to the library to read up on elephants. We'll meet again at lunch recess on Monday."

When Monday came, the Copycats and Pearl Hotchkiss all noticed how often Thekla Mustard brought up the story of the Six Haunted Hairdos, and how the Tattletales all smirked and tried to hide their smiles behind their hands. It was deeply annoying. But the problem of a ghost elephant was more urgent. Revenge would just have to wait.

At lunchtime Stan Tomaski and the other Copycats huddled with Pearl Hotchkiss near the gym door. "Have we got news for you!" Sammy Grubb told Stan.

"And I have something to tell you, too," said Stan.

Sammy Grubb went first. He told Stan about the trick the Tattletales had played on them, and about the ghost elephant, and about Salim's fear that the spirit of Baby Tusker had come all the way from Bombay to seek revenge on him.

Stan gulped and then said, "Well, I have another theory, gang."

"What is it?" said Sammy.

Stan told them about the Cohoes Mastodon. "I wasn't there to see the ghost you saw," he said, "but would you say it looked sort of shaggy? As if it had long hair, like an Angora kitten?"

"Exactly," said Hector. "I thought it was the blurred outlines of the Holi powder, but maybe it was long hair."

"That's what I think!" said Pearl excitedly. "When I went back to the library, Mr. Dewey found me a book called *Elephants in History*. The woolly mammoth, a distant cousin of the mastodon, was a prehistoric elephant that roamed this part of North America. It had a sloping back like the one we saw. Salim, maybe what we saw wasn't Baby Tusker! Maybe it was the ghost of a woolly mammoth!"

"But why would a ghost of a woolly mammoth suddenly start haunting Hardscrabble Hill?" asked Moshe Cohn. "I mean, after all these thousands of years? Why now?"

"We need to think about this," said Sammy Grubb. "Something very important is happening. You know what we need?"

"Absolutely," said Salim. "A chocolate swoon doughnut. You know, I have begun to enjoy their delicate chocolate flavoring. Quite scrumptious, indeed. Perhaps I am truly becoming American."

After school the Copycats and Pearl hurried off to Grandma's Baked Goods and Auto Repair Shop. Grandma Earth was just finishing up with the town snowplow. She was touching up a few rust spots on the blade with rust remover. She put her brush down and took off her orange gloves and came to the bakery case.

"Nobody on the CB radio has heard about these haunted hairdos," said Grandma Earth, "but everyone in town is buzzing about them. Should I be afraid to bring logs in from the woodpile once it gets dark?"

"I don't really think you need to worry, Grandma Earth," said Sammy. "But while you're getting us eight chocolate swoons, could I ask you a question?"

"Ask away, I don't charge to listen, I only charge for answering," said Grandma Earth, but she was only kidding. Half the time she didn't even charge for doughnuts; that's how nice she was.

"Hamlet may well be haunted," said Sammy, "but not by Six Haunted Hairdos. I think there's something else going on, something quite earthshaking."

"What do you mean?" said Grandma Earth.

Sammy explained their theory about a woolly mammoth haunting Hardscrabble Hill.

Grandma Earth nibbled a chocolate swoon doughnut to give herself mental strength. "Your use of the word *earthshaking* is interesting," she said. "Perhaps you mean even more than you realize. Maybe the dynamiting has woken it up."

They all stared at her. No wonder Miss Earth was such a brilliant teacher. She had such a brilliant mother. Brilliance must drip through the Earth family genes like clarified butter.

"Well, everyone in Hamlet has heard these loud booms all month," said Grandma Earth. "Didn't the marble quarriers move to a new vein of rock this autumn? That's why they've been dynamiting, to open it up and get it ready for cutting. Maybe the explosions blasted right in the place where the woolly mammoth had died, so the slumbering ghost arose. Maybe down at the bottom, underneath the earth, the ghost of a woolly mammoth has been lying at peace for all these years. And now it's been woken up."

"But," said Forest Eugene, radiating an air of caution like a true scientist, "out of all the thousands of animals and mosquitoes and birds that have died in that location over the last ten million years, why did only an elephant wake up?"

"I'm not sure if I believe in ghosts," said Grandma Earth, "but my daughter, Germaine, says that if they exist, they are the spirits of creatures who have died unhappily. So maybe this woolly mammoth got caught in a mud pit or something and died in sorrow. Now it's awake and it is looking for what it needed and wanted on the day it died."

Pearl spoke up. "The ghost came to Old Man Fingerpie's farm. That's what I saw on Halloween: its trunk reaching for the peanuts in my trick-or-treat bag. I wonder what it *does* want?"

"Good question," said Hector. "It came to my house, too. But what was it looking for? A glass of warm milk so it could go back to sleep for another fifty thousand years?"

"Who can say?" said Grandma Earth. "But doesn't it make a kind of sense? That it's looking for what it wanted on the day it died?"

It did, especially to Salim, who was so relieved that the ghost might not be the ghost of Baby Tusker that he glowed with joy.

"So let's keep our eyes open," said Sammy. "Now that we've made friends with that ghost, sort of, maybe it'll tell us what it wants."

"I'm not sure all ghosts are scary," said Grandma Earth. "Frankly, I'm more scared of Mayor Grass, who's coming to pick up the snowplow today. Snow predicted before long, you know, and I'm not quite done with the rust removal. Kids, if you are going to fool around with ghosts, be careful."

"Thanks, Grandma Earth," said Sammy. "We will."

They left the shop and stood outside. "Let's go back up there," said Pearl. "Before too long the ground will be covered with snow and it will be hard to hike up Hardscrabble Hill."

"Agreed," said Sammy Grubb.

The Copycats and Pearl Hotchkiss stopped at the general store and bought a sack of peanuts. Then they climbed Hardscrabble Hill again. They couldn't wait to locate their friend the ghost elephant. For a few minutes they stood, looking down at their beloved Hamlet. It was hard to believe a small village in Vermont was being haunted by the ghost of a woolly mammoth. Life sure was surprising sometimes.

"Look," said Hector. "You can see my house, where the back porch used to be before we had it removed." (An elephant ghost can do a lot of damage when it is being bulky and full of body instead of smoky and weightless. Even if it is friendly.)

"Hey, look," said Sammy Grubb. "Can you see over on that slope there? Below the bluff that has the pine trees all in a green and black mass there? See the clearing just below that?"

It took a minute or two for them to focus their eyes. But when they did, their jaws dropped.

The wind on that far slope was stirring up leaves. The leaves were massing together in the air, filling in the ghostly vessels, turning visible what by rights should remain invisible.

It wasn't just one ghost elephant.

There were more. There were three, four, five—no, six. It was a small congress, a tribe, a herd of woolly mammoths congregating beneath the pines. The tops of the trees shook as the elephants passed beneath the bare branches, greeting each other, raising their trunks and entwining them.

The wind died down suddenly. The leaves fell. The ghosts became invisible again, unfilled, unformed. But when last seen they had been turning to follow the leader—a pinkish one, larger than the others—up the far slope of Hardscrabble Hill.

"I think we've had one boom too many," said Sammy in a sober voice. "The whole family's awake now. Folks, we better figure this out soon, before all of Hamlet is overrun with ghosts."

17
Spelling It Out

The Copycats were sure that the explosions at the marble quarry had awoken the elephant ghosts. The only problem was finding out what the elephant ghosts wanted. As friendly and welcoming as Vermont was, a population of phantom woolly mammoths could cause a bit of a problem.

At school on Wednesday, the last day before the Thanksgiving holiday, Sammy Grubb raised his hand. "Miss Earth," he said, "do you think that we kids ought to tell the grownups that we have *actually seen* ghosts?"

"Everybody should hear about the Six Haunted Hairdos!" interrupted Thekla, and all the Tattletales snickered.

"We wouldn't want unsuspecting motorists to get in an accident by being frightened by a passing ghost," said Miss Earth. "On the other hand, we don't want to cause needless worry. If those were ghosts you saw, perhaps they are just passing through."

"Passing through!" said Thekla. "That's a good joke. Ghosts are always *passing through* things when they are passing through! Miss Earth, you're a stitch!"

"But what if they stay?" said Sammy Grubb. "Think of the reputation Hamlet would get. A ghost town!"

"If I recall the ghost stories told around the fire at Girl Scout camp, and I believe I do," said Miss Earth, "all ghosts lurk in their ghostly way because there is some unfinished business in their past. Something they need, something they want. Maybe it's revenge. Maybe it's to warn the living. Maybe it's to scare them. Or maybe it's love. Don't jump to conclusions."

"I wonder what the Six Haunted Hairdos want?" said Thekla, winking at her friends. "Maybe they want to fall in love with any available *boys*." At this all the Tattletales roared with laughter. With great dignity the Copycats ignored them.

"If I should meet a ghost," said Miss Earth, "I should be inclined to ask it politely how I might be of service. Courtesy counts, my dears, even in the spirit world."

"Boo unto others as you would have them boo unto you?" gasped Thekla, tears of laughter streaming down her face.

"Thekla, you should be on the Comedy Channel," said Miss Earth, "which, by the way, I never watch and I never will. Now, Salim, tell me, is your family going to make a turkey and cranberry sauce?"

"My mom found a recipe for turkey curry," said Salim. "We're having that."

"Bravo, and a very happy Thanksgiving to you all," said Miss Earth as the children got their winter coats. "Enjoy the parades on TV, enjoy your families, and don't forget to be grateful for what you have."

"On behalf of the entire class, may I say that we're grateful for *you*, Miss Earth," said Pearl Hotchkiss.

"And I for all of you," she answered.

The Josiah Fawcett Elementary School was dismissed for the Thanksgiving vacation at lunchtime. The Copycats and Pearl Hotchkiss once again found themselves trudging up the slope of Hardscrabble Hill. "Now that I know this isn't Baby Tusker," Salim said, "I feel much braver. I think that Miss Earth is right. We should try to find out what these woolly mammoths want. Maybe we can help."

"I don't believe anyone here speaks Woolly Mammoth," said Pearl.

"We'll have to improvise," said Sammy. "Babies don't understand words, but they know an awful lot of what you're saying. So do dogs and cats. Maybe ghostly elephants will too. Let's try it."

When they got to the oak grove halfway up Hardscrabble Hill, they paused to scatter some peanuts on the ground.

Before long there was a sense of airy motion. The leaves from the forest floor whirled up and assumed the shapes of six huge, hulking woolly mammoths.

"Remember my rules about ghosts," Salim said softly to the others.

"If you see a ghost, first pinch yourself to make sure you're awake," whispered Sammy Grubb.

"Here I go," said Salim and pinched himself on the butt. "Ouch. Yes, I am awake."

"Next, pinch the ghost to see if it's really there," said Sammy Grubb.

Salim reached out to the shimmery rope of leaves and twigs that seemed to be the trunk of the foremost woolly mammoth. Salim cupped his hand and moved it gently up and down a ridge of air, patting the invisible skin. "It feels like the scratchy underside of a carpet," he said in a low, trembly voice.

"If it pinches back," said Sammy Grubb, "run for your life."

But the elephant didn't pinch back. The Copycats and Pearl could see it reach out its trunk and settle it gently on Salim's shoulders, curling it about his neck with affection and kindness.

"What do you want?" asked Salim. "Can you show us what you want?"

The leaf-drawn woolly mammoth pulled back. It seemed to nod. With an almost inaudible sigh, it turned and headed up the track to the old swimming hole. The boys and Pearl followed, and the other woolly mammoths trooped along after them. It was a strange parade of kids and fallen autumn leaves.

When the group reached the swimming hole, the lead woolly mammoth paused and held Salim and the others back with its trunk. Then the six ghosts lumbered over to the other side of the water. Now that the kids knew what they were looking at, they gasped. The leaf-cloaked elephants could still be "unseen"—that is, you could scramble your eyes and tell yourself you were just seeing unusual atmospheric conditions. But when you looked in the reflection in the pond, there was no denying what you saw. Six huge, hairy, sober-looking, upside-down mammoths, with long brown tresses and arching tusks.

"What do you want?" asked Salim again.

The six elephants all shook themselves. The leaves that gave them form flew away and they were invisible again, except in the reflections. But the leaves all fell onto the surface of the pond. The lead woolly mammoth put her trunk in the water—by now they were sure it was a she, though for reasons no one could name—and she began to stir the leaves into a pattern. A couple of other woolly mammoths joined in. They were making a picture out of the leaves on the surface of the water.

"What is it?" breathed Pearl Hotchkiss.

"Baby Tusker?" said Salim Bannerjee.

"It *is* a baby elephant!" said Pearl. "That is what they want!"

And so it seemed to be. The brown leaves had been nudged into an outline of a little elephant with a huge head. A flaming yellow leaf had been deposited right in the center of the head, so it looked like an elephant profile with one bright eye alert and watching. The trunk curled forward as if reaching for something.

"What happened?" said Pearl. "Did you all die while trying to protect your little baby from some attacking dinosaur or something?"

"We'll help you to find your baby," said Sammy Grubb stoutly. "Is that what you'd like us to do?"

The lead woolly mammoth nodded—that is to say, her reflection in the water nodded.

"I have a plan," said Sammy Grubb. "In fact, I have two plans. We'll come back here tomorrow morning when we're ready to help you. But if we help you, Will you help us?"

The elephants didn't exactly nod, but there was a real feeling of understanding across the water of the pond.

"What are you talking about?" said Salim. "How are we going to find the elephant baby that these ghost woolly mammoths are looking for?"

"I have had a brainstorm," said Sammy Grubb. "In fact, two of them. We need to talk. Let's go regroup on the stone wall by Old Man Fingerpie's farm."

They said good-bye to the woolly mammoths and tramped down to the meadows of Old Man Fingerpie's farm.

"Well," said Sammy, "*some* of the mystery is cleared up now. This mama elephant has been hunting for her baby. When she came to Old Man Fingerpie's house, she saw Pearl. Maybe she likes human kids because she misses her own elephant child. When she came to Hector Yellow's house, she wanted to get inside to be with us."

"Dad said it was a lightning bolt that hit the

porch," Hector reminded them, being loyal to their new ghost friends.

"So," said Sammy, "I have a plan. If we can only lure the ghost of Baby Tusker here, Salim, we can introduce it to the ghost woolly mammoths! They'll have their baby to take care of, Baby Tusker will have a new family, and when the ghosts get what they want, they will silently slip away and stop haunting us!"

"Easier said than done," said Salim. "I thought that the ghost of Baby Tusker was following me on the Air India jet. But then it got locked in the overhead luggage compartment. It's been a good four months since then. I don't know where it is now."

"How come it didn't just float out through the door of the luggage compartment?" said Pearl.

Forest Eugene explained about H_2O having the forms of water, vapor, and ice, and that ghosts could probably do that too. "Maybe it was too anxious to change back, or it couldn't manage it with everyone so agitated."

Sammy Grubb said, "Salim, your ghost has probably been changing planes, back and forth across America. Waiting in various airport lounges for connecting flights! Haunting the information booths, looking for you! Maybe we could have every airport in America page him! 'Paging Baby Tusker! Paging Baby Tusker! Please pick up the white courtesy phone!'"

"I don't know why that doesn't seem very realistic to me," said Salim. "It's an interesting idea and all, but I think it won't work."

"Well, what ideas do *you* have?" said Pearl.

"I spent the last couple of weeks hoping I wasn't being haunted by Baby Tusker," said Salim. "It's hard suddenly to hope that Baby Tusker does show up. I'm not so good at such fast changes."

High up, an airplane was crossing the sky, maybe making the commuter flight from Montreal to Hanover, New Hampshire.

"Look at these fields in Old Man Fingerpie's farm," Pearl said suddenly. "Suppose we wrote a sign in stones? 'Welcome Baby Tusker' or something. Then if the ghost was in an airplane flying overhead, it might look down and see it, and come down."

"I doubt ghosts can read," said Salim.

"It's worth a try," said Sammy. "You know, as a gesture of welcome. Maybe Baby Tusker has been trying to reach you, Salim, but maybe it's scared. Maybe that's why it didn't come out of the overhead luggage compartment. Maybe it's been following you, but at a distance. Maybe it just needs a gesture of welcome to encourage it. I think a message saying 'Welcome Baby Tusker' might just do it."

"We'll help," said Moshe, and the other boys nodded.

"I don't have any other ideas," Salim admitted. "Why not?" He was glad his new friends all wanted to help.

18
Return of the Six Haunted Hairdos

So the Copycats and Pearl Hotchkiss hurried over to one of the well-mowed fields in Old Man Fingerpie's farm. It didn't take them long to tug stones into big lines, six feet long, that read WELCOME BABY TUSKER! from one edge of the field to the other. While they worked, they sang a song, just in case Baby Tusker could hear with its ghostly ears. After all, real elephants were supposed to have wonderful hearing. Maybe Baby Tusker was lonely and needed to be sung to. Another way to make it feel welcome.

Pearl made up a lullaby based on a country-and-western song that Miss Earth often hummed to herself. Pearl substituted the word *elephant* for *truck driver's*. It went like this:

> *Honey, baby, elephant child,*
> *Someone loves you deep and wild.*
> *I've a dozen states and a week to go,*
> *So I'm callin' your name on the CB radio.*

After they sang that forty-seven times into every direction, Sammy Grubb told them about his second brainstorm.

"It's one thing to bring together prehistoric woolly mammoth ghosts and an orphaned present-day baby elephant ghost," said Sammy. "But we also have to deal with the low trick the Tattletales played on us—dressing up as Six Haunted Hairdos and scaring the living daylights out of us! It's time to get back at the Tattletales. And we've got the goods to do it."

"What do you mean?" asked Hector Yellow.

"Here's what we need," said Sammy Grubb. "We need a whole lot of Holi powder. Salim, how much can you get your hands on?"

"Lots," said Salim. "My parents imported tons of it to sell, but there isn't much demand for it in Vermont."

Sammy Grubb said, "For this plan to work, we need some paint, lots of old newspapers, some metal coffee cans, and a dozen cans of hair spray. We need some bright cloth cut up in eight-inch strips, about three feet long each. We need a portable tape player and a tape of Petunia Whiner singing 'Stick with Your Man.' We need five cardboard boxes, some duct tape, some black plastic garbage bags, the largest size they have. We need a pair of hedge clippers. We need a couple of matching coffee-table lamps. We need a rake."

"But what is the plan?" asked Pearl. "I don't get it."

"Come nearer, everyone," said Sammy. The

Copycats and Pearl Hotchkiss formed a huddle, and Sammy Grubb whispered his idea. He said it in a very low voice so that he couldn't possibly be overheard by anyone outside the circle, even an invisible eavesdropping ghost.

"We need to have our heads examined," said Pearl Hotchkiss. "This will never work."

"Are you with us, Pearl?" asked Sammy Grubb.

"I'm not a Copycat," Pearl reminded them. But then she remembered Thekla's nasty words to her on the playground. "As long as nobody gets hurt, I guess you can count me in. But I'll be amazed if we pull it off."

"The Tattletales put one over on us," said Sammy Grubb. "Now it's our turn. But not a word to a soul except the eight of us. We don't want anyone to figure out our secret plan before we unveil it!"

They worked like the dickens for the rest of the afternoon and the evening. Pearl went over to Thekla Mustard's house to lay the trap.

Thekla Mustard was surprised to see Pearl standing on her front porch. "What excess of Thanksgiving spirit brings you here for a visit, Pearl?" she asked. "Are you here to join the Tattletales at last? If you did, the girls' club would outnumber the boys' club."

"Thekla," said Pearl, "on Hardscrabble Hill this afternoon I saw the Six Haunted Hairdos again."

Thekla's eyes narrowed. Were her Tattletales out

parading in their costumes without her permission? "Is that so?" she said warily. "And why are you coming to tell *me* about it?"

"Well," said Pearl, "the girls in Miss Earth's class—you and your loyal subjects—say that you don't believe in ghosts. I thought that if your Tattletales came to Hardscrabble Hill tomorrow morning, maybe the Six Haunted Hairdos would appear again. Then the Tattletales could see them the way you did and believe in ghosts themselves."

Thekla pondered. Had the boys figured out the trick played on them? Were they trying to get even? "Where will the Copycats be tomorrow morning?" she asked suspiciously.

"They'll be there," said Pearl.

Thekla thought hard. If the Tattletales came—as themselves—then there was no chance of the imaginary Six Haunted Hairdos showing up. The boys would be humiliated again. What a nice way to celebrate Thanksgiving. "All right," she said. "I'll round up my club members. We'll meet at Old Man Fingerpie's farm at 8 A.M. sharp. I'd hate to miss the Macy's Thanksgiving Day Parade on TV."

Before she went home, Pearl Hotchkiss stopped at Grandma's Baked Goods and Auto Repair Shop.

Grandma Earth was just about to close up shop. Miss Earth was helping her rebuild a carburetor. "Why Pearl, what are you doing here?" said her teacher.

"Grandma Earth," said Pearl, "could you do me a favor?"

"If I can," said Grandma Earth.

"Could you send out a message on your citizen's band radio?" said Pearl. "Say, 'Calling Baby Tusker, calling Baby Tusker: Hamlet, Vermont, is waiting for you.' And ask all your friends on the airwaves to broadcast that same message?"

"That's the oddest message I ever heard," said Grandma Earth. "What do I do if Baby Tusker answers? And who is Baby Tusker anyway?"

"I can't tell you who Baby Tusker is. It's sort of a secret. And I don't think you'll get an answer," said Pearl. "But if you broadcast it, maybe somewhere, somehow, Baby Tusker will hear it."

"Pearl, for you, anything," said Grandma Earth. "Do you want a chocolate swoon doughnut to eat on your way home?"

"No thanks," said Pearl.

"A raspberry ruffle? A prune popover? A cranberry cruller? A blueberry bun? A mango muffin?"

"No, no, no, no, and no. I'm not hungry. But, I wonder, Miss Earth: Do you happen to have a tape of Petunia Whiner singing 'Stick with Your Man'?"

"As a matter of fact, I do," said Miss Earth. "Seems to be a very popular tape these days. Thekla Mustard borrowed it a few days ago but just returned it."

"Hmm," said Pearl. "Why am I not surprised. Good-bye, Miss Earth. Good-bye, Grandma Earth. Have a nice Thanksgiving. And thanks a lot." She tucked the tape in her pocket.

Pearl was just about to leave when Miss Earth said, "Pearl?" The girl turned. Her teacher held out a heart-shaped cookie with a pilgrim's hat painted in frosting on it. "My mother has told me some of the theories about the ghosts on Hardscrabble Hill," said Miss Earth. "Remember one thing always, Pearl. Ghosts hang around because they are unhappy. Only love can heal a haunting."

Pearl took the cookie to be polite, even though she wasn't hungry. She ate it on the way home and thought about what Miss Earth had said. Only love can heal a haunting. How did Miss Earth know that? Did Miss Earth have personal experience in this department?

Was Pearl being haunted by Sammy Grubb? He wasn't even dead. Interesting thought.

Only love can heal a haunting. Sounded like a country-and-western song.

At seven o'clock on Thanksgiving morning, the Copycats and Pearl Hotchkiss met at Old Man Fingerpie's farm. They were lugging all the supplies that Sammy Grubb had ordered them to get. It was a tough hike up the hill, but when they were high enough up to look back, they would see the stone letters, shining with a white frost, gleaming like metal down in the field. WELCOME BABY TUSKER!

It was very gratifying. Any ghost flying overhead would see it. Maybe ghosts had a kind of mental telepathy and could broadcast the message about.

Baby Tusker should show up any minute. They just hoped Baby Tusker didn't come before they had finished their trick.

As soon as they got to the oak grove, they scattered the peanuts and waited.

It took less than a minute for the six ghost woolly mammoths to emerge from the forest. When the six elephants were dusted with Holi powder, they looked like six punk rocker elephants with shaggy dyed-pink hair.

"Okay, gang," said Sammy Grubb, holding up a lock of the first elephant's long straggly hair, "on to the next stage!"

At eight o'clock, when the Tattletales arrived, the Copycats were waiting for them in the field. "Where's Pearl?" asked Thekla suspiciously. "This was all her idea."

"She called me this morning," said Sammy Grubb. "She has an evil stomach virus. She can't make it."

"Hmmm," said Thekla. "Well, let's get this over with. Today is our national holiday of gratefulness, and I would be furious to have to take too much time away from being grateful."

"Be grateful if we get to see any of the Six Haunted Hairdos," said Sammy Grubb.

"I'll be very grateful," said Thekla. "But somehow I doubt it's going to happen." And she and all the Tattletales giggled.

"We saw them once," said Sammy. "Those odd

ladies from the fall foliage tour. You can't deny that, Thekla. You were right there with us."

"I don't recall," said Thekla. "My life is so busy and interesting, I can't keep details like that in my head."

"I don't believe there were any ghost ladies," said Anna Maria, trying to keep a straight face.

"Complete nonsense," agreed Sharday.

"Who could swallow such a yarn?" said Nina.

"It's all in your heads, you superstitious boys," said Carly.

"Bet we don't see a thing," said Lois.

"Absolutely," said Fawn. "Except maybe for Jack Frost painting ice patterns on the pond with his little magic paintbrush."

Everybody looked at her. "Doesn't anyone else believe in Jack Frost?" she asked faintly.

They all shook their heads sadly. Fawn began to sniffle. "Fawn," said Thekla, "if you see a balloon of Garfield the Cat in the Macy's Thanksgiving Day Parade, remember: It's just a balloon."

They passed through the oak grove and headed up the slope toward the swimming hole.

"Now be very quiet," said Sammy Grubb. "If the Six Haunted Hairdos are here, they will be scared by shrieking."

"What a waste of time," said Thekla, yawning.

"Easy . . . easy does it . . ." muttered Sammy Grubb.

The wooded patch on the opposite side of the swimming hole seemed to tremble in the thin

November morning light. A few feet off, a stand of thick pine trees shivered, though no wind could be felt on this side of the water.

"Six Haunted Hairdos!" called Sammy Grubb softly. "We're here!"

For a minute nothing happened.

Then Thekla's mouth dropped open. "Oh my aching eyeballs . . . " she cried out.

From behind the stand of pines came Pearl Hotchkiss, leading Six Haunted Hairdos. "Look what I found!" she said brightly. The Haunted Hairdos were swaying and lumbering along. They were huge heads without bodies, gently bumping along on the ground. The heads were twelve feet high and eight feet wide. The hair was shocking pink. It stood up like a Mohawk, or it was curled, or braided, or frizzed out. One Hairdo had a hat. One had a huge set of sunglasses and a buzz cut. One had ribbons tied in huge bows. One had a little flip. All of them moved side to side to the tune of "Stick with Your Man."

"*Aaaahhhh!*" screamed Thekla Mustard.

"*Aaaahhhh!*" screamed the Tattletales.

Nina and Carly grabbed each other's waists. Sharday and Lois clutched each other's necks. Anna Maria and Fawn twisted each other's fingers. Thekla Mustard, the Empress of the Tattletales, said, "It's like the giant balloons from the Macy's Thanksgiving Day Parade, but they're not in Herald Square—they're here. Six Haunted Hairdos! Girls, what have we done! May I suggest that we all—"

"Run for your lives?" said Salim gently.

"Run for our lives!" bellowed Thekla. And they raced down the side of Hardscrabble Hill as if ghosts were after them.

Pearl Hotchkiss helped Sammy Grubb take the huge pair of sunglasses off one of the woolly mammoths. The frames had been made out of cardboard boxes and the lenses out of black plastic from garbage bags. Hector combed out the curls of one woolly mammoth. Forest Eugene took the huge paper hat off another. Stan untied the ribbons from the woolly mammoth with braids. Mike undid the braids. Moshe patted down the spiky part of one elephant's hairdo, which had been shaped by the hedge clippers and six cans of hair spray. Salim stood there in front of all of them and said to the ghosts, "You've all done very well. How can we show you our thanks?"

The lead elephant pointed to the water. "Yes, yes," Salim said, "I know. Your baby. We're working on that. Give us another day or two."

But in fact, they didn't have to wait one more day. Because when Pearl and the Copycats got down to the bottom of the hill, they were greeted by the surprise they'd been waiting for.

19
Baby Tusker

At the edge of the field huddled Thekla Mustard and the Tattletales. Beyond them stood an elephant ghost, just a little one, maybe five feet tall. It was more visible than the woolly mammoths—maybe because it hadn't been a ghost for so long. The ghost was a milky gray, with tender eyes and a bashful glance.

"It's Baby Tusker!" said Sammy Grubb. "Isn't it, Salim?"

Salim came forward. His heart was in his throat. It was all his fault! Baby Tusker must hate him!

But Baby Tusker saw Salim and capered forward in a sprightly way. It lifted its trunk and touched Salim's face. It curled its trunk around Salim's neck like a scarf. It nuzzled its great gray ghostly head against Salim's shoulder.

"It likes you," said Pearl Hotchkiss.

"It is a ghost," said Thekla Mustard. "Is it related to those Haunted Hairdos we just saw up by the swimming hole?"

Pearl turned around and stared coldly at Thekla Mustard. "There never were any Haunted Hairdos. You made that all up," she said. "There never was a fall foliage tour minivan that crashed into the swimming hole. I looked it up in the library. No such thing. Thekla, you were just trying to humiliate the Copycats for believing in ghosts!"

"I thought I was making it up, but maybe I was mind-reading it!" Thekla said coolly. "Because what about the Six Haunted Hairdos we just saw? You saw them as well as I did!"

At this, Pearl started laughing, and so did all the Copycats—everyone except Salim, who was being hugged by Baby Tusker. "Hah!" laughed Sammy Grubb. "Hah. Hah! Our little plan worked!"

"You engineered this, Sammy Grubb!" screamed Thekla Mustard.

"Don't flip your wig," chuckled Sammy Grubb. "We only did to you what you did to us. Of course there's no such thing as Six Haunted Hairdos."

"Then what are those things we saw? Giant Muppets from outer space?" screamed Thekla.

"No," said Sammy Grubb seriously, "those are ghosts."

"Well, at least we girls got scared by *real* ghosts," said Thekla. "You boys got scared by disguises. That makes us superior, as usual."

Thekla was being brassy, but the other girls looked ashamed. "Look," said Lois to Sammy, "maybe we did play a nasty trick on you. We're sorry. We didn't know there were real ghosts hanging around. It was Thekla's idea."

"A good one, too," said Thekla sharply. "And it worked."

"Thekla," said Sammy, "we are going to have to put our little contest on hold. We have a real problem here. Are you willing to work together with us?"

"I don't know," said Thekla in a pouting voice.

"If Thekla won't lead the Tattletales in a collaboration with you, I will," said Lois loudly.

"Of course I'll do my part as Empress of the Tattletales," snapped Thekla. "Lois, back off. You're always on the make. Okay, Sammy Grubb, state your business."

Sammy Grubb quickly told the Tattletales the theory about where the ghost woolly mammoths came from and what it was they were looking for.

"Well, that's easy enough," said Thekla Mustard. "Here's a ghost baby right in front of our eyes. We can introduce them."

"Easier said than done," said Sammy Grubb. "This is Baby Tusker. He has followed Salim here all the way from India to haunt him."

"Oh," said Thekla.

They all watched Baby Tusker nuzzle and lick and sniff Salim Bannerjee.

"That's an awfully friendly kind of haunting," observed Pearl.

"I think it likes me," said Salim. "But I can't keep a ghost elephant in my bedroom. I'm not allowed to have pets."

"Why should it like *you*?" asked Thekla, sulking. "*I* found it."

Sammy Grubb told the Tattletales about the untimely death of Baby Tusker, back in a zoo in Bombay. "Salim thinks it's his fault," said Sammy, "but judging by the amount of lovey-dovey going on over there, I think he's gotten his story wrong. I think that Baby Tusker was so glad to be fed that it fell in love with Salim. That's why it's been chasing him all this time. Not to haunt him. So that Salim can be its mother."

"I can't be its *mother*!" said Salim.

"Let me," said Thekla bossily and pushed forward. But Baby Tusker was a timid ghost and hid behind Salim, whimpering.

"Well, one thing's clear," said Pearl Hotchkiss. "This baby elephant needs a family. And that family of ghost woolly mammoths up there is looking for a baby. Maybe if we introduce them to each other, they will all get what they want and stop hanging around Hamlet. Only love can heal a haunting. As Miss Earth says. It would make a nice Thanksgiving-type happy ending, don't you think?"

"Pearl is right," said Sammy Grubb. "Let's bring Baby Tusker up to the old swimming hole. This is a family reunion just waiting to happen. Salim, if you lead Baby Tusker, will it follow?"

"I'll try," said Salim. He walked a few steps. Baby Tusker stepped briskly along behind him, ears flapping gently in the wind.

"Well, let's go then," said Sammy. "But everyone, be quiet. We don't want to frighten away the ghost woolly mammoths."

It was just a short walk back up through the oak grove to the swimming hole. There Pearl Hotchkiss went to the edge of the water and called out, "Yoo hoo! Boo who! Where's a Haunted Hairdo?"

The Copycats had taken off the most outlandish parts of the ghost elephant disguises. Still, when the six woolly mammoths appeared, in their pink curls and braids and spiky hair, they looked more than awesome.

"Look, Baby Tusker," said Salim gently. "Here's your new family." When Baby Tusker turned to look, Salim stepped away nimbly from his ghostly friend. He didn't want to interfere in a ghost bonding session. He wanted the ghosts to deal with each other without his getting in the way.

The lead mammoth raised her trunk and sniffed the air. For a minute she looked expectant. Her eyes widened, and something almost like a smile crossed her big pink face.

But then her nose went down. Her forehead went down. She shook her head slowly, slowly. She wandered off, and the others followed her.

"This is awful!" cried Pearl.

"She knows it's not her real baby," said Sammy. "I just realized—her real baby probably survived the death of its mother and its tribe. It probably grew up and maybe even emigrated across the Bering Strait, back to Asia, maybe as far as India. That's why this ghost mama mammoth can't find her baby! Her baby lived to be a big old elephant and died thousands of miles away. Maybe it was even an ancestor of Baby Tusker."

"We have to push a ghost adoption through here!" said Thekla. "But how can we convince her that Baby Tusker needs her?"

"Baby Tusker is scared of her," said Salim. "Look." Baby Tusker was busy trying to hide itself behind a birch tree.

"This is terrible," said Lois. "Salim, drag that baby over there."

"I can't do that," said Salim. "It's terrified."

"Well," said Thekla Mustard, "I suppose there's only one thing to be done."

"Yes?" said Sammy.

Thekla said, "This poor baby elephant must be terrified of those pink monster hairdos. And who could blame it? It's also been chasing around airports for months trying to find its way here. It's exhausted and sick with worry. There's only one way to get those elephants all together and start behaving like a family."

"And what way is that?" asked Sammy Grubb.

"We've got to scare them out of their wits," said Thekla smartly. "It sounds mean, but it's the only thing that'll make them band together. I think this sorry situation calls for a return of the Six Haunted Hairdos."

She looked out over the Tattletales. "Girls, are you ready to give your all for the sake of a happy elephant ghost family?"

"Yes!" they cried.

"Wait," said Pearl Hotchkiss, stepping forward. "Now, you Copycats. Come on, you Tattletales. Listen to me."

"What?" said Sammy Grubb.

"I don't listen to anyone just because I'm commanded to do so," said Thekla sharply, but the other Tattletales crowded in front of Pearl and chorused, "What, Pearl? What?"

"Miss Earth said that only love can heal a haunting," said Pearl. "So I don't think we better do any more pretend haunting. We've had enough of trying to scare each other, or anyone else."

"Why trust Pearl? She's hardly—" began Thekla. But both the Copycats and the Tattletales were sending Thekla such haunted looks that she fell silent—perhaps for the first time in her life.

"Oh, all right," said Thekla. "What's your big fat idea, Pearl?"

"I think that we need some ghost family therapy in a crisis like this," said Pearl. "We have to give them something to love together."

"Like what?" said Thekla, sulking. "You mean like a pet?"

"Why not?" said Pearl. She looked slyly at Thekla. "You're not volunteering by any chance, are you?"

"No thanks," said Thekla. "I have other plans for my career, namely to be the first woman to be President of the United States, President of the United Nations, and President of the United Tattletales of America—all at the same time. I have no time to devote to being a ghost pet. Salim got us into this mess. If anyone, it should be Salim."

"No!" cried the Copycats.

"No!" cried the Tattletales.

"No!" cried Pearl.

"Well, it was just an idea; don't get so edgy," said Thekla.

But Salim Bannerjee was standing there with a funny expression on his face. He almost looked as if he were going to cry.

"I didn't know you liked me that much," he said.

"Oh well, we're Americans, we can't help it, we like everyone," said Thekla. "You'll get used to it. But I take back my suggestion, Salim. I don't really want to give you away to some ghosts. You're pretty neat. I mean, for a boy, which isn't saying much."

Salim gulped a couple of times and said, "Well, what can we do, then? If we're not going to be Haunted Hairdos and haunt the ghosts? And if we're not going to give one of ourselves up to be the pet of a ghost? What does Miss Earth mean, 'Only love can heal a haunting'?"

"I'll explain it to you," said Miss Earth.

20
Only Love Can
Heal a Haunting

Miss Earth and her mother emerged from the path through the woods. Grandma Earth was huffing and puffing a bit and leaning on a walking stick. She had a sack of chocolate swoon doughnuts knotted in a scarf that she wore on top of her head. She looked a little bit a Haunted Hairdo herself, only she smelled like chocolate heaven.

While Grandma Earth caught her breath, Miss Earth said, "I began to be a little worried about the things I'd been hearing about Haunted Hairdos. And then when Pearl Hotchkiss came by yesterday and asked my mother to put out an all-points bulletin calling for Baby Tusker, I got a little alarmed. I called Mr. Dewey in the library and asked him to go on-line on the library computer. I gave him the words *Baby Tusker* as a clue. Mr. Dewey did some internet surfing and some web crawling and some e-mail SOSing. Somebody in Bombay who apparently had insomnia answered his questions.

Baby Tusker was a poor little elephant child who died of an evil stomach virus. I began to wonder if the ghost of Baby Tusker had followed Salim from Bombay to Hamlet, Vermont."

"Miss Earth," said Sammy Grubb, "may I say for once and for all, you are one genuine chocolate swoon."

"Miss Earth," said Thekla Mustard, not to be outdone, "it behooves me to congratulate you on your superior brains, which, I point out, are entirely female, thank you very much."

"Miss Earth," said Pearl Hotchkiss, "you are right on the money. There's the ghost of Baby Tusker." She pointed to the edge of the clearing.

"I don't believe in ghosts," said Grandma Earth, rubbing her eyes, "and even *I* can see it. Cute thing. I wonder if it would like a job plowing the roads of Hamlet this winter? Looks stronger than the town's old snowplow." But she was only kidding.

"Miss Earth," said Pearl, "didn't you say that only love can heal a haunting?"

"That's correct," said Miss Earth. "And I should know."

"What do you mean?" said Pearl.

Miss Earth looked embarrassed. "It's rather private."

"We'll keep the secret," said Pearl. "Promise."

"Once," said Miss Earth, "I was in love. With a wonderful man from Manhattan. And he was in love with me. We were to be married the day after Thanksgiving, right here in Hamlet. But unfortunately, on his way to Grand Central Station to come to Vermont, he was carrying such a huge armload of flowers for the wedding that he couldn't see where he was going. He walked out into the middle of the Macy's Thanksgiving Day Parade. Alas, he was run over by the float carrying Santa Claus. All the elves cried themselves sick. And so did I."

"And so did I," murmured Grandma Earth. "That sad, sad day."

"And were you haunted by him?" asked Pearl Hotchkiss in a soft voice.

"Not in a traditional sense," said Miss Earth. "That is, I never saw his ghost. No. But he was in my mind day and night. I missed him and loved him and could hardly think of anything else. That's a kind of haunting too, you know. And I was haunted by him for a long time, until love came to rescue me."

"But where did love come from? Who loved you so much?" cried Salim. "That is, if it's not impolite to ask," he added.

"It wasn't who loved me," said Miss Earth, "for I have always had wonderful people to love me, starting with my father and mother. My dear mother kept loving me as hard as she ever had." She smiled at Grandma Earth. "No, children, the love that heals a haunting is the love that you can give to others. And I started to give my love away again when I started teaching at the Josiah Fawcett Elementary School."

"You fell in love with Jasper Stripe, the janitor?" screeched Fawn Petros.

"No, Fawn," said Miss Earth. "I fell in love with

you, my students. And loving you healed me. I don't expect you to understand now. Maybe when you're older."

But each and every one of the children felt they understood perfectly. And they felt quite proud about it, too, and nudged each other and mumbled and blushed. "We love you too, Miss Earth," said Salim Bannerjee boldly.

"This is getting entirely too mushy for me, and the doughnuts are getting too mushy, too," said Grandma Earth, opening up her bundle. "Let's all have a little chocolate swoon and think about what to do next."

The children had each taken a bite of doughnut when something rustled in the grass at their feet. They all looked down. Miss Earth turned pale.

"I hope it's not a mouse," she said.

Forest Eugene adjusted his eyeglasses and peered over the tops of them. "I do believe," he said, "it is the ghost of a mouse. It seems to be the ghost of Jeremiah Bullfrog."

Hector Yellow gasped and leaned down on his hands and knees. It was the ghost of a mouse. It looked like a little smudge of brownish gray air twitching on the leaves.

"Oh, Jeremiah Bullfrog!" cried Hector. "You've come back to say good-bye!"

The ghost of Jeremiah Bullfrog looked around with an interested expression. It sort of floated up onto Hector's open palm and nuzzled for a second.

"Do you want to take it home with you?" asked Miss Earth.

"I can't," said Hector. "We got a new cat named Dogfood. Because that's what she eats and that's what Daddy says she's going to be if she doesn't watch out. She'd gobble up a mouse ghost and burp little haunted hairballs."

"Then say good-bye," said Miss Earth, "and let it go. You've found something new to love. Only love can heal a haunting, Hector."

Hector said good-bye. There were some damp eyes watching. Then Jeremiah Bullfrog the mouse wafted in a skittering sort of way over toward Baby Tusker.

At first Baby Tusker seemed afraid. Its ears went up and its trunk snaked about looking for Salim. Salim wanted Baby Tusker to look for comfort elsewhere, so Salim just stood behind Grandma Earth, who was stout enough to hide him from Baby Tusker's view.

Miss Earth began to sing in that charming, completely tuneless way she had. She sang,

> Blizzards snow, tornadoes blow,
> Ingrown toenails come and go.
> Troubles grow, but even so,
> Ghost, here's what you gotta know:

Miss Earth drew her breath in, smiled at her mother, and warbled,

> Stick with your mom!

The children began to sing the second verse:

> *Earthquakes shake, fires bake,*
> *Every waking heart can break.*
> *Don't you make a big mistake.*
> *Ghost, come on, for goodness' sake:*
> *Stick with your mom!*

Baby Tusker seemed to respond to the inspired words of Petunia Whiner, that country-and-western music singer extraordinaire. Baby Tusker twisted about and careered across the field, right into the middle of the circle of ghost woolly mammoths. The tiny ghost of Jeremiah Bullfrog chased eagerly after it.

> *Showers pour, hurricanes roar,*
> *Your hairdo looks like it's been in a war.*
> *Pimples make your skin so sore.*
> *But ghost, remember what you're for:*

The Copycats, the Tattletales, Pearl, and Miss Earth chimed together,

> *Stick with your mom!*

The ghost woolly mammoths looked worried. They closed ranks around Baby Tusker and turned their backs to it. But this wasn't being mean. This was to protect it. The ghost mammoths lowered their heads and looked fiercely at Jeremiah Bullfrog as if daring the ghost mouse to come any closer.

Jeremiah Bullfrog stopped. "Only love can heal a haunting," whispered Miss Earth.

Baby Tusker whimpered with worry. The mother woolly mammoth reached out, almost by habit, and chucked Baby Tusker under its chin. Baby Tusker nuzzled up underneath her, standing in the shadow of her great shaggy jaw. She curled her trunk against the elephant child and closed her eyes.

Now that Baby Tusker was safe, it could look at Jeremiah Bullfrog.

"Come on, what's to be scared of?" said Forest Eugene. "It can't hurt you."

Baby Tusker regarded Jeremiah Bullfrog solemnly. The little mouse scurried up its trunk and sat on the curving end of it. Baby Tusker, being safe under the chin of the elephant mother, was now brave enough to make a friend of Jeremiah Bullfrog.

"Our work here is done," said Thekla Mustard softly. "Happy Thanksgiving, everybody."

Sammy smiled at Pearl. "Thanks for helping," he said. "You're a true friend."

"Look," said Salim. Everyone turned toward him. He smiled, spreading out his arms. He seemed to be a little sad and a little happy at the same time. "Look, everybody. It's starting to snow. My first snow ever."

21
Over the Hills
and Far Away

The Copycats and the Tattletales shook hands with
each other. "A Thanksgiving truce," said Thekla
Mustard. "We have to hand it to you fellows. You
proved that there *are* such things as ghosts."

"And you were good sports to help us out," said
Sammy Grubb. "But if we ever see Six Haunted
Hairdos again, we'll know the three things to do."

"What?" said Thekla.

"Pinch ourselves to make sure we're awake."

"And the second thing?"

"Pinch the Haunted Hairdos to make sure we're
not imagining them." Sammy Grubb stopped.

"And the third thing?" asked Thekla Mustard
impatiently.

"If they pinch back," said Sammy Grubb, "we'll
run for our lives!"

The children chased one another all the way down
Hardscrabble Hill, trying to pinch one another.
Grandma Earth and Miss Earth followed a little

more slowly. At the bottom of the hill, Miss Earth reminded them that ghosts might be fun to meet now and then, but it was still better to be alive. They should all be thankful, especially since it was Thanksgiving Day.

"Yes, Miss Earth," they all said and headed to their homes. Thekla ran on ahead so she wouldn't miss any of the Macy's Thanksgiving Day Parade.

When Pearl had said good-bye to her friends, she skipped along the margin of Route 12 because she felt so happy. Sammy Grubb had said a special thanks to her. His smile was so cute. That was what she was grateful for.

She thought about it some more. Only love can heal a haunting. It wasn't really true that her heart was being haunted by Sammy Grubb. It wasn't that serious. It was just that she liked him—liked him a lot. She wasn't in love with him. And he sure wasn't in love with her. And that was just fine all around. It was just the way it should be. Plenty of time for lovey stuff in the future. When she was Miss Earth's age.

She was so pleased with realizing this that she made up her own country-and-western chorus.

You are just Sammy and I am just Pearl.
A boy's just a boy and a girl's just a girl.
When all of this fighting about who's better ends,
What's better than being just old-fashioned friends?

She sang it all the way home.

When the Thanksgiving dinner of turkey curry was but a spicy memory and the pans were soaking in the sink, Salim said to his parents, "Are you glad we moved to Vermont from Bombay?"

"We miss Bombay," said his mom. "But we like it here. As long as we're together, we're happy."

"Besides," said his dad, "the long-distance phone rates are low today, because it's a holiday. So I called your grandparents in Bombay. Guess what they told me? Remember that elephant baby we saw at the zoo? Remember the one that died after we saw it?"

"Yes?" said Salim cautiously.

"Well, today in the Bombay *Times* was an article that said the zoo got a new elephant, and that elephant got sick too. It turns out that the problem wasn't an evil stomach virus. It was something in the water that didn't have anything to do with what the elephants ate. So you don't have to worry about feeding Baby Tusker those peanuts. The peanuts wouldn't have hurt it at all."

"Oh," said Salim. But he had stopped worrying already, once he had finally met up with Baby Tusker again. He could tell that Baby Tusker hadn't wanted to blame him for anything. Baby Tusker had been so glad to be fed something by someone kind— especially since its mother had already died—that Baby Tusker had been lonely for him. That's why the ghost of Baby Tusker had followed him into the Air India jet in Bombay.

After dinner, Salim wrapped himself in three sweaters and a scarf to keep warm, and he went out walking—not down toward Hamlet, but higher, higher, higher. Past Old Man Fingerpie's farm, past the oak grove, past the swimming hole in the old quarry. Up to the brow of Hardscrabble Hill, from where the beginning of the Green Mountains stretched in white and silver and brown folds, up to a white horizon.

He could see them now. He could see them clearly. The swirling gusts of snow were filling the woolly mammoths in, just as richly as the Holi powder had. Only they looked better white than pink. They looked more like themselves.

They ambled along, wild mountain elephants with their long hair, their daggerlike tusks, and their swaying trunks. The mother was in the lead and the others followed. Like elephants trained in the circus, they seemed to be linking themselves together, tail to trunk, trunk to tail. Baby Tusker was the last, holding on tightly. If Jeremiah Bullfrog was with them, it was too small to be seen.

Salim hurried, from tree to tree, watching, as the snow thickened and the beasts grew whiter and denser. It was almost as if they were carved out of blocks of Hamlet marble. They shuffled in a family procession, taking care of each other, counting each other, watching each other, and listening for danger. Being grateful for each other.

When they got to the open brow of Hardscrabble Hill, where the soil had been scrubbed off the rock by centuries of wind, the mammoths stood for a moment. They were an entirely visible chain, a

Thanksgiving Day Parade all of their own. From the valley below you'd be able to make out only snow against the sky. But Salim, behind a pine just at the tree line, watched with longing and fascination.

For a moment, Baby Tusker let go of the tail in front of him. The baby elephant ghost turned and waved at Salim, its trunk straight out like a military salute. Salim waved back.

The mother raised her trumpet and made a blast—like thunder, like a sonic boom, like a quarry detonation. Whether she was calling the wind or saying good-bye to Salim, he could not decide. Then a wind from the north came rushing down, as if in response to a summons, and the ghost elephants swirled in a gust of snow, and were gone.

Author's Note

I am not an expert on ghosts. I only saw one once, in Paris. It was wearing a yellow straw hat and playing a guitar near a sidewalk café. It didn't get near enough for me to ask it any questions. Consequently, for the purposes of this book, I've had to make up a few things about the spirit world. Artistic license, you know.

Readers, however, may be interested to learn that from the 1920s to the 1980s there actually was a life-size model of the Cohoes mastodon. It was on display in the State Museum of New York at Albany. I remember as a small boy seeing the thing, monumental as an archbishop, holding court at the far end of the long display corridor on the third floor (I think) of the State Education Building. This mammoth model inspired *Six Haunted Hairdos*.

I'm told that when the State Museum changed location, the model of the mastodon was installed in the Cohoes Public Library. With the kind of artistic license that pleasingly resembles absolute power, I imply in *Six Haunted Hairdos* that the mastodon is still in Cohoes. However, in real life the model of the Cohoes mastodon is no longer with us. It suffered badly in a hot sort of accident involving two little boys and a match. I don't know the names of those two boys, but I hope they're being haunted by a huge elephant ghost.